FROM *THE NEW YORK TIMES:*

"Nick Carter has attracted an army of addicted readers . . . the books are fast, have plenty of action and just the right degree of sex . . . they take the reader away from the dullness of his everyday life to a world that has mystery and excitement . . . Nick Carter is the American James Bond, suave, sophisticated, a killer with both the ladies and the enemy."

Now . . . follow the espionage adventures of Nick Carter in this taut, tense thriller—BEIRUT INCIDENT.

"NICK CARTER OUT-BONDS JAMES BOND."

—*Buffalo Evening News*

"Nick Carter is the oldest surviving hero in American fiction. In his latest Killmaster incarnation, he has attracted an army of addicted readers for the Nick Carter series that has been published in a dozen languages, from Dutch to Japanese. . . . Nick Carter is super-intelligence par excellence . . . [his] penchant for sex and violence seems to have universal appeal."

—*The New York Times*

"America's #1 espionage agent."

—*Variety*

"Generation after generation of readers has been drawn to Nick Carter."

—*Christian Science Monitor*

"Nick Carter has emerged as America's most popular, most resilient and most imitated fictional character! . . . Nick Carter is extraordinarily big."

—*Bestsellers*

*Dedicated to The Men of the
Secret Services of the
United States of America*

A Killmaster Spy Chiller

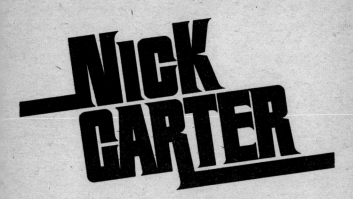

NICK CARTER

BEIRUT INCIDENT

CHARTER
NEW YORK

A DIVISION OF CHARTER COMMUNICATIONS INC.
A GROSSET & DUNLAP COMPANY

BEIRUT INCIDENT

CHAPTER 1

The wind was hot and dry on my face, parching my lips in the 130-degree Saudi Arabian heat. For the third time I brushed my fingers reassuringly across the searing butt of Wilhelmina, my 9mm Luger. If I ever caught up with Hamid Raschid and the Dutchman, I wanted to make sure she hadn't been jolted out of the spring-loaded shoulder holster I wore under my bush jacket. The potholes on that two-lane strip of macadam that twisted across the desert were teeth-rattling.

I gripped the wheel harder and pressed the little Jeep accelerator to the floor. Reluctantly, the speedometer needle edged up toward seventy.

The shimmering desert heat waves distorted my vision, but I knew that somewhere down the highway ahead of me was the big SAMOCO truck I was chasing.

Hamid Raschid was a cunning Saudi, small, dark, thin-boned, a homosexual. He was also a sadistic killer. I remembered the mutilated body of one of the oil line guards we had found in the desert just three days before.

Sometimes you have to kill, granted. But Hamid Raschid enjoyed it.

I squinted through my sunglasses and tried to will more speed from the Jeep. Coming up in the distance were a group of the towering, wind-swept sand dunes that dot the Saudi wasteland, interspersed with stark, hard-packed rocky ridges not unlike the mesas of Arizona.

If I didn't overtake the truck before we reached the dunes, there would be an ambush waiting for me somewhere along the thirty-seven-mile stretch of road between Dhahran and Ras Tanura. And Hamid Raschid knew he'd been flushed. Before the day was over, one of us would be dead.

The Dutchman. In his own way, the amiable, blond-bearded Dutchman—Harry deGroot—was as deadly as Raschid. The breakdown on the Dutchman had come through just the night before in a coded message from AXE, America's elite counterintelligence unit:

> DeGroot, Harry, 57. Dutch collaborator. Dep-
> uty Director, Enhizen, 1940-44. East Germany,
> saboteur, 1945-47. Turkey, Syria, Jordan, Saudi
> Arabia, espionage, 1948-60. Romania, saboteur,
> 1961-66. USSR, espionage instructor, 1967-72.
> Education: University of Gottingen, geology.
> Family: None. Rating: K-1.

K-1 was the key. In AXE's cryptic style, it meant "ruthless and professional." K-1 was equivalent to my own Killmaster rating. Harry deGroot was a well-trained assassin.

The geology background, of course, explained why he had been posted in the Mideast.

Raschid, too, was an oil expert. His studies fifteen years

before at the American University in Beirut had dealt primarily with petroleum exploration. It is an ever-popular subject in that part of the world.

It was also what had brought me to Saudi Arabia on a Priority One urgent assignment from AXE. It had started innocuously enough on April 17, 1973, when, according to *The New York Times,* "unknown saboteurs tried to blow up the Saudi-American Oil Company's pipeline in southern Lebanon."

Explosive charges had been set off under the pipeline four miles from the Zahrani terminal, but little damage had been done. Initially, that bungled attempt at sabotage was written off as just another harassment by Yasir Arafat's Palestine Liberation Front.

But that turned out to be only the first of a long series of incidents. They weren't aimed at disrupting America's flow of oil. The October, 1973, War and the ensuing boycott by the Arab states had already done that. The goal was to cut off Western Europe's flow of oil, and the United States couldn't afford that. We needed a strong, economically expanding Western Europe to offset the power of the Soviet bloc, and the oil that kept the NATO nations alive came from Saudi Arabia. So even though we weren't getting the oil ourselves, the American oil companies in the Arab countries were committed to keeping our Western Allies supplied.

When terrorists leveled the oil depot at Sidi Behr, my irascible boss at AXE, David Hawk, called me in.

My job, Hawk told me, was to get the ringleaders, cut the plant off at the roots. It had been a long trail, leading through London, Moscow, Beirut, Teheran and Riyadh, but now I had them—racing ahead of me down the highway toward Ras Tanura.

The truck was getting closer now, but so were two towering sand dunes and a rocky ridge leading off to the right. I leaned forward to keep my desert-parched face behind the small windshield of the Jeep. I could see beyond the lurching blue shape of the big stake truck to the sharp curve in the highway, where it disappeared between the dunes.

I wasn't going to make it.

The truck hurtled into the curve at high speed and disappeared between the dunes. I cut the Jeep's ignition so that only the sound of the truck's laboring engine could be heard in the silent heat of the desert.

Almost immediately that sound, too, was cut off, and I slammed on the brakes, skidding half off the road before I came to a stop. Raschid and the Dutchman had done just as I had suspected they would. The truck was stopped now, probably broadside to the road. Raschid and the Dutchman would be racing to the shelter of the rocks on either side of the road, hoping I would come slamming into the blockading truck.

I wasn't about to. Hidden by the bend in the road, just as they were, I sat for a moment in the Jeep, considering my next course of action. The sun hung brightly in the cloudless sky, a relentless ball of fire baking the shifting desert sands. Sitting still now, I could feel the sweat running down my chest.

My mind was made up. I swung my legs out of the Jeep and moved quickly to the foot of the towering sand dune. In my left hand I carried the jerry can of extra gasoline that was standard equipment on every SAMOCO vehicle in the desert. In my right hand was the canteen that was usually hooked in its bracket under the dashboard.

By now, Raschid and the Dutchman, anticipating a big crash—or, at least, my wildly careening effort to avoid one—would have realized that I was on to them. Now they would have two choices: either wait for me, or come after me.

I calculated they would wait: The truck provided a natural barricade and the road, with dunes on either side, served as a deadly funnel to feed me right into the muzzles of the two AK47 rifles which had been strapped under the seat of the truck cab. To circle the dune on the left would take an hour, maybe more. The dune on the right, banked up against a long finger of rock, would be impossible to drive around. It extended for miles.

There was only one other way to go—up and over the top. But I wasn't sure I could make it. The sand dune looming above me stood more than seven hundred feet high, rising precipitously with sides carved out steeply by *schamaals,* the searing desert wind storms that sweep the red-brown Saudi wasteland.

I needed a cigarette, but my mouth was as dry as parchment already. Crouching at the foot of the dune, I drank hungrily of the brackish water in my canteen, letting it sluice down my throat. I poured the remainder over my head. It ran down my face and neck, soaking the collar of my bushjacket, and for one grand moment I felt the relief from the insufferable heat.

Then, quickly unscrewing the top from the jerry can, I filled my canteen with gas. When I put the top back on the canteen I was ready to go. I hooked it onto my belt and started up.

It was incredible. Two steps up, one back. Three up, two back, sand sliding out from under my feet, throwing me face down against the burning slope, the sand so hot it blistered my skin. My hands clawed at the steep pitch, then jerked away from the scorching sand. This wouldn't work—I couldn't climb the dune going straight up. The running sands wouldn't support my footholds. To move at all, I would have to stretch, spread-eagled on the slope in order to gain maximum adhesion; but to do so meant burying my face in the sand, and the sand was too hot even to touch.

I twisted around to lie on my back. I could feel the nape of my neck beginning to blister. The entire dune seemed to be pouring under my bush jacket and down my pants, caking on my sweating body. But on my back, at least, my face was out of the sand.

Lying backward on that mountain of sand, I began to inch my way uphill slowly, using my arms in wide sweeping motions and my legs in froglike kicks. It was as if I were swimming on my back.

The bare power of the sun beat at me implacably. Between the sun pouring out of that trackless sky and the reflected heat of the sand, the temperature as I struggled up the hill must have been around 170 degrees. According to the Landsman Ratio, desert sand reflects roughly one-third of the heat of the surrounding air.

It took me a full twenty minutes before I reached the crest, panting, dehydrated, thirsty, and covered with sand. Cautiously, I peered over the top. If either the Dutchman or Hamid Raschid happened to be looking in my direction, they would spot me in an instant, but it would be a difficult shot for them, shooting upward.

It was just as I had figured. There was the truck, angled crossways across the road, both doors open. Hamid Raschid, a small figure in his white *galibeah* and red-checkered *kaffiyeh,* trotted from the side of the road back toward the truck, and positioned himself so that he could aim down the road through the open doors of the cab.

The Dutchman had already taken up a defensive position underneath the truck, protected by the big rear wheel.

I could see the sun glinting on his glasses as he peered around the overblown sand tire, his white linen suit and striped bow tie incongruous against the battered body of an aged truck in the empty desert.

Both men were concentrating on the highway. They weren't expecting me at the top of the dune.

I leaned back behind the protection of the crest and got ready for action.

First I checked Hugo, the stiletto I always wear in a chamois sheath strapped to my left forearm. One quick twist of my arm and Hugo can be in my hand.

I eased Wilhelmina out of her holster and checked the action, making sure she wasn't clogged by sand. An exploding Luger would rip a gunman's hand from his wrist. Then I took the Artemis silencer from my bush jacket pocket and carefully brushed the sand from it before fitting it over the muzzle of the pistol. I wanted the extra precaution of the silencer so I'd be able to get off three or four shots before Raschid and the Dutchman realized where they were coming from. The bare explosion of the Luger would give my position away prematurely.

There was one more operation to perform before I was ready to go into action. I unscrewed the top from the canvas-covered canteen, twisted my handkerchief into a six-inch rope and jammed it into the spout. My mouth and throat were rasping dry. Without water I wouldn't last five hours in that desert heat, but I had good reason for replacing the water with gasoline. The canteen now made a fine Molotov cocktail.

I lit the makeshift wick and watched with satisfaction as the gasoline-permeated handkerchief began smouldering. If I could get far enough down the slope before I threw it, the sudden motion of the actual throwing should slosh enough gasoline out of the mouth of the canteen to explode the whole thing. But if my descent turned into a wild plunge down that slope of sliding sand, the gasoline would slosh out of the can while I held it—and it would explode in my hand. I said a silent prayer and set my smouldering bomb in the sand beside me.

Then I rolled over on my stomach in the blazing sand and inched my way to the crest, keeping as flat as I could, Wilhelmina extended before me.

I was ready.

Hamid Raschid and the Dutchman were still in place, but they must have been getting restless, wondering what I was up to. The sun glinted off Raschid's rifle, extended out the open door of the cab, but I could see nothing of Raschid himself except a small patch of the red and white checkered *kaffiiyeh* he wore on his head.

The Dutchman offered a better target. Crouched down behind the rear wheel of the big truck, he was at a bit of an angle to me. Part of his back, his side and his hip were exposed. Shooting downhill through shimmering heat waves didn't make him the world's best target, but it was all I had.

I sighted carefully. A lucky shot would crush his spine, a very good one would smash his hip. I aimed for the spine.

I squeezed the trigger slowly and deliberately.

Wilhelmina bucked in my hand.

Sand spurted at the Dutchman's feet.

Involuntarily, he jerked backward, partially upright. That was a mistake. It made him a better target. The second shot hit him, and he spun halfway around before he dived again for the cover of the truck wheel. The third shot kicked up more sand.

I cursed and put my fourth shot through the cab of the

truck. A lucky ricochet just might put Raschid out of action.

I was up and over the crest of the hill now, plunging, sliding, half up to my knees in pouring sand; I was straining to keep from pitching forward in the loose footing, with Wilhelmina clutched in my right hand, and my canteen firebomb in the other, held gingerly aloft.

Three shots from Hamid Raschid's rifle thundered in the desert stillness. They spat into the sand ahead of me in rapid succession. The range wasn't too bad, but a man lurching downhill from above is an almost impossible target. Even the finest marksmen in the world will invariably shoot low in such circumstances, and that's what Raschid was doing.

But now I was closing in and nearing the bottom of the hill. I was within thirty yards of the truck, but still I could not see Raschid as he fired again through the open doors of the cab. Bullet-wind ripped at the pocket of my bush jacket.

Twenty yards now. The ground was suddenly level, and much harder. It made running easier, but it also made me a better target. A rifle boomed to my right, then again. The Dutchman had gone back to work.

Now I was fifteen yards from the cab of the truck. The muzzle of Raschid's AK47 extended across the front seat spouting flame. I threw myself to the right and onto the hard-baked ground just a half second before a bullet whined overhead.

As I went down to my knees, I swung my left arm in a long, looping arc, lofting the canteen firebomb gently into the cab of the truck.

It landed perfectly on the seat, tumbling across the barrel of Raschid's rifle toward the wiry Saudi.

It must have been only inches from his dusky, high-boned face when it exploded in a roaring geyser of flame. One earsplitting shriek of agony ended eerily, cut off at the high crescendo as Raschid's lungs turned to ash. I was already moving, leaping for the shelter of the big SAM-OCO truck hood.

I leaned against the heavy front bumper for a minute, gasping for air, the blood pulsing in my forehead from super-exertion, my chest heaving.

It was the Dutchman and me now. Just the two of us playing cat and mouse around an old blue stake truck in the middle of the empty Saudi Arabian desert. Only a few feet away I could smell the acrid stench of burning flesh. Hamid Raschid was no longer a player in this game, only the Dutchman.

I was at the front of the truck, exhausted, winded, covered with sand, frying in my own sweat. He was nicely positioned behind the rear wheel of the truck. He was wounded, but I had no way of knowing how badly.

He was armed with a rifle. The chances were also damned good that he had a pistol. I had Wilhelmina and Hugo.

There were only two choices open to each of us: Either stalk the other or sit and wait for the stalker to make the first move.

I knelt quickly to peer under the truck. If he were moving, I would be able to see his legs. He wasn't. The tiniest bit of pant leg, just a glimpse of white linen, peeked out from behind the right wheel.

I removed the silencer from Wilhelmina for better accuracy. Holding onto the bumper with one hand and leaning almost upside down, I squeezed off a careful shot at the scrap of white.

At best, I might get him on a ricochet or perhaps even cause a blowout that would startle him enough to break cover. At worst, it would let him know exactly where I was, and that I knew where he was.

The shot reverberated in the silence as if we were in a small room rather than one of the emptiest spaces in the world. The tire wheezed air and slowly flattened, canting the big truck over at an awkward angle toward the right rear. The net result was that the Dutchman had a slightly better barricade than before.

I stood up against the heavy grill and counted back. I had fired four shots so far. I would much rather have a full clip, no matter what happened. I fished some shells out of my bush jacket pocket and began reloading.

A shot rang out, and something nudged the heel of my shoe, sand spurting up out of nowhere. I jumped, startled. I cursed myself for being careless and leaped onto the bumper of the truck in a half crouch, keeping my head below the level of the hood.

The Dutchman could shoot under trucks, too. I was lucky. If he hadn't been shooting from an extremely awkward position—as he must have been—he could have cut my legs out from under me.

For the moment I was safe, but only for the moment. And I couldn't remain clinging to that unbearably hot metal hood much longer. Already my body felt like it had been charcoal broiled.

My alternatives were limited. I could drop to the ground and lie there, to peer under the truck and wait for the Dutchman to make his move, hoping for a shot at him underneath the chassis. Except that with his rifle, he could reach around the protecting wheel and pretty well spray any vantage point I might choose without exposing much of his body.

Or else, I could hop down off that bumper and leap into the clear on the left, so I would have a full view of the man. But no matter how I jumped, I would land somewhat off-balance—and the Dutchman would be kneeling or prone, and steady. He had only to move the muzzle of his rifle a matter of inches for a dead-on shot.

If I went the other way, circling the truck and hoping to catch him by surprise from the other side, he would shoot the legs out from under me the moment I moved in that direction.

I took the only other route open to me. Up and over. With the Luger in my right hand, I used the left as a lever and clambered onto the radiator hood, then up to the cab roof, to drop silently to the bed of the truck. With luck, the Dutchman would be fairly low in the sand behind the deflated right wheel, his attention riveted on the space under the truck bed, waiting for a glimpse of me.

There was no shot, no flurry of movement. I had apparently made my move undetected.

I peered through the space between the slats of the high-staked truck bed. Then, slowly, I crept across to the right rear corner of the vehicle.

I took a deep breath and stood up to my full six-feet-four so that I could look down over the top slat of the sideboards, Wilhelmina at the ready.

There he was, spread-eagled at an angle from the wheel, flat in the sand on his belly. His cheek was firm against the stock of the rifle—the classic prone position for marksmanship.

He had no idea I was there, just three feet above him, staring at his back.

Carefully, I raised Wilhelmina to chin height, then extended my arm over the side of the upper slat of the truck. I aimed at the back of the Dutchman's neck.

He remained motionless, waiting for the first sign of

movement that he could spot underneath the truck. But I wasn't coming that way. He was as good as dead.

I squeezed Wilhelmina's trigger.

The gun jammed! Goddamned sand!

Instantly, I shifted my weight from my left foot to my right and snapped my arm downward to release Hugo. The stiletto slid neatly into my left hand, its pearl handle hot to the touch.

There was no way Hugo could jam. I grasped the knife by the haft and cocked my arm, holding the stiletto ear-high. I usually prefer a blade-throw but at this distance, with no interval for the standard end-over-end flip, it would be a haft-throw, straight down, three feet, right between the shoulders.

Some sixth sense must have warned the Dutchman. He suddenly rolled over on his back and stared up at me, his AK47 arcing toward me as his finger began the trigger squeeze.

I snapped my left arm forward and down.

The needle point of the stiletto pierced the Dutchman's staring right eyeball and drove its three-sided razor-sharp blade into his brain.

Death twitched the saboteur's finger, but the shot echoed harmlessly in the desert sand.

For a moment I hung on with both hands to the top slat of the truck, my forehead pressed against the back of my knuckles. My knees suddenly felt very shaky. I'm fine in action, well-trained, never hesitant. But after it's all over, I always get a very shaky, nauseated feeling.

In one way I'm very normal. I don't want to die. And each time there's the flood of relief that I got them and it wasn't the other way around. I took a deep breath and went back to my work. It was just routine now. The job was over.

I retrieved my knife, wiped it clean, and returned it to its forearm sheath. Then I examined the Dutchman. I had hit him in that wild shooting charge down the hill, all right. The bullet had ranged along the right-hand rib cage. He had lost a lot of blood and it must have been painful, but it was hardly a crippling wound.

It didn't really matter, I thought to myself. What did matter was that he was dead and the job was over.

There was nothing of importance on the Dutchman, but I transferred his wallet to my pocket. The boys in the lab might learn something interesting from it.

Then I turned my attention to what was left of Hamid Raschid. I held my breath while I made a distasteful search of his clothes, but found nothing.

I stood up, fished one of my gold-tipped filter cigarettes out of my bush jacket pocket and lit it, figuring out my next move. Just leave things as they were, I finally decided, inhaling the smoke gratefully despite the parched condition of my mouth and throat. I could send a *sadiki* crew back to pick up the truck and the two bodies once I returned to Dhahran.

Raschid's red checked *kaffiyeh* caught my eye and I kicked at it with the toe of my shoe, flipping it over in the sand. Something gleamed, and I leaned over to examine it more carefully.

It was a long, thin metal tube, much like the sort of thing that expensive cigars are packed in. I took off the cap and peered at it. Looked like granulated sugar. Wetting the end of my little finger, I tasted the powder. Heroin.

I replaced the cap and balanced the tube in my palm thoughtfully. About eight ounces. It had been, undoubtedly, Raschid's payoff from the Dutchman. Eight ounces of pure heroin could go a long way toward making an *emir* out of a beggar in the Middle East. I stuck it in my hip pocket and wondered how many of those tubes the Arab had received in the past. I'd send it back to AXE. They could do what they wanted with it.

I found Raschid's canteen in the front seat of the truck and drank it dry before tossing it aside. Then I climbed into the Jeep and headed back down the highway to Dhahran.

Dhahran hung low on the horizon, a dark green silhouette about eight miles down the road. I pressed harder on the accelerator. Dhahran meant cold showers, clean clothes, a tall, cool brandy and soda.

I licked dry lips with a parched tongue. A day or two more to get my reports in order and I'd be out of this hellhole. Back to the States. The fastest route would be by way of Cairo, Casablanca, the Azores, and finally, Washington.

Not one of those cities would rank with the garden spots of the world, but I had plenty of time coming to me if David Hawk didn't have an assignment ready and waiting. He usually did, but if I took my vacation in bits and pieces all along the route home, there wouldn't be much he could do about it. I just had to make sure I didn't accept any telegrams or cables along the way.

In any case, I thought, there's no point taking the dry-throat non-fun route. I'd go home the other way, by way of Karachi, New Delhi, and Bangkok. After Bangkok, what? I shrugged mentally. Kyoto, probably, since I have never cared much for the smog and clamor of Tokyo. Then Kauai, the Garden Island of Hawaii, San Francisco, New Orleans and finally, Washington, and an undoubtedly furious Hawk.

Before all that, of course, there was still tonight—and probably tomorrow night—in Dhahran. Muscles tightened involuntarily, and I grinned to myself.

I'd met Betty Emers just a week ago, her first night in Dhahran after having been in the States on a three-month vacation. She had come into the club at about nine o'clock one night, one of those women with such a sexual aura that somehow, in that special, subtle way, communicated the message to every man at the bar. Almost in unison every head in the place turned to see who had come in. Even women looked at her, she had that kind of presence.

I'd been attracted to her at once, and she hadn't sat alone at her table more than five minutes before I walked over and introduced myself.

She'd scanned her dark eyes over me for a brief second before she returned the' introduction and invited me to join her. We'd had a drink together and talked. I learned that Betty Emers was an employee of one of the American-owned oil companies—and I learned that her life in Dhahran had lacked an important element: a man. As the evening progressed and I found myself becoming more drawn to her, I knew that that would soon be remedied.

Our evening ended with a night of furious lovemaking in her small apartment, our bodies unable to get enough of each other. Her deeply tanned skin was as soft as velvet to the touch, and after we'd spent ourselves, we'd lain quietly, my hand gently caressing every inch of that wonderfully smooth skin.

When I had to leave the next day, I did so with reluctance, showering and dressing slowly. Betty had wrapped a wispy robe about her, and her farewell had been a hoarse, "See you again, Nick." It had not been a question.

I thought now of her perfect body, the flashing eyes, her short black hair, and I felt her full lips under mine when I'd taken her in my arms, crushing her to me as we lingered long and deep over a farewell that promised more delights to come . . .

Now, driving down the Ras Tanura road in a hot, dusty Jeep, I was sweaty again. But it wasn't the same. I grinned to myself as I drove through the Dhahran compound gate. It soon would be.

I stopped at the security office and left word with Dave French, SAMOCO's chief security officer, where to pick up Raschid and the Dutchman. I brushed off his congratulations and desire for details. "I'll give it all to you later, Dave, right now I want a drink and a bath, in that order."

What I really wanted, I told myself as I climbed back into the Jeep, was a drink, a bath, and Betty Emers. I had been too busy with Hamid Raschid and his gang to have spent more than a few phone calls with Betty since that first night. I had a little catching up to do.

I halted the jeep outside my Quonset hut and clambered out. Something was wrong.

As I reached for the doorknob I could hear the strains of Bunny Berrigan's "I Can't Get Started" coming through the door. That was my record, all right, but I certainly hadn't left it playing when I went out that morning.

I pushed open the door, furious. Personal privacy was the only surcease from the steaming cauldron of Saudi Arabia and I was damned if I would see it violated. If it was one of the *sadikis,* I told myself, I'd have his hide, but good.

With one motion, I threw open the door and stormed in.

Lounging comfortably on my bed, a tall, glistening drink in one hand and a half-smoked cheap cigar in the other was David Hawk, my boss from AXE.

CHAPTER 2

"Good afternoon, Nick," Hawk said calmly, his grim-visaged New England countenance as close to a smile as he ever allowed. He swung his legs around and came to a sitting position on the side of the bed.

"What on earth are you doing here?" I stood in front of him, towering over the small, gray-haired man, my legs spread defiantly, arms akimbo. Forget Karachi. Forget Delhi. Forget Bangkok, Kyoto, Kauai. David Hawk wasn't there to send me off on vacation.

"Nick," he admonished quietly. "I don't like to see you lose control of yourself."

"Sorry, sir. A temporary lapse—the sun." I was still seething, but contrite. He *was* David Hawk, a legendary figure in counter-espionage, and he *was* my boss. And he was right. In my business, there is no place for a man who loses emotional control. You either retain your control at all times, or you die. It's as simple as that.

He nodded amiably, the foul smelling cigar firmly

clamped between his teeth. "I know, I know." He leaned forward to peer at me, squinting slightly. "You look awful," he observed. "I gather you've finished the SAMOCO thing."

There was no way he could have known, but somehow he did. The Old Man was like that. I strode over and stooped to examine myself in the mirror.

I looked like the sandman. My hair, usually jet black with just a few flecks of gray, was matted with sand, and so were my eyebrows. The left side of my face was a stinging pattern of scratches, as if someone had worked me over with coarse sandpaper, caked with a dried mixture of blood and sand. I hadn't even realized I'd been bleeding. I must have scraped myself worse than I'd thought scrabbling up the sand dune. For the first time, also, I realized my hands were tender from pressing them against the hot metal of the truck out in the desert.

Ignoring Hawk, I threw off my bush jacket and slipped out of the holsters that held Wilhelmina and Hugo. Wilhelmina would need a thorough cleaning, I thought to myself. I quickly got rid of my shoes and socks and then stepped out of my khaki pants and shorts, all in one motion.

I headed for the shower in the back of the Quonset hut, the sharp coolness of the air conditioner icy on my skin.

"Well," Hawk commented, "you're still in good physical shape, Nick."

Complimentary words from Hawk were really rare. I tightened my stomach muscles and surreptitiously stole a glance downward at my bulging biceps and triceps. There was a puckered reddish-purple depression on my right shoulder, an old gunshot wound. A long, ugly welt ran diagonally across my chest, the result of a knife fight in

Hong Kong years ago. But I could still press over six hundred pounds, and my records back at AXE Headquarters still carried "Top Expert" classifications in marksmanship, karate, skiing, horsemanship, and swimming.

I spent a full half-hour in the shower, soaping, rinsing, and just letting the icy spikes of water blast the grime off my skin. After I had toweled myself vigorously, I donned a pair of khaki shorts and rejoined Hawk.

He was still puffing away. There might have been a hint of humor in his eyes, but there was none in the coldness of his voice.

"Feel better now?" he asked.

"I sure do!" I filled a snifter to the halfway mark with Courvoisier, added a single cube of ice and the barest splash of soda. "All right," I said resignedly, "What's up?"

David Hawk took his cigar from his mouth and squeezed it between his fingers, staring at the smoke curling up from the ash. "The President of the United States," he said.

"The President!" I had a right to be surprised. The President almost always kept out of AXE affairs. Although our operation was one of the most sensitive in the government, and certainly one of the most vital, it also often overstepped the bounds of morality and legality that any government must, at least on the surface, espouse. I'm sure the President was aware of what AXE did and, to some small degree at least, aware of how we did it. And I'm sure he was appreciative of our results. But I knew, too, that he'd rather pretend we didn't exist.

Hawk nodded his crew-cut head. He knew what I was thinking. "Yes," he said, "the President. He has a special assignment for AXE and I'd like you to handle it."

Hawk's unblinking eyes pinned me to my chair. "You'll have to start right away . . . tonight."

I shrugged my shoulders in resignation and sighed. Goodbye, Betty Emers! But I was flattered I'd been chosen. "What does the President want?"

David Hawk permitted himself the ghost of a smile. "It's sort of a lend-lease deal. You'll be working with the FBI."

The FBI! Not that the FBI isn't good. But it's not in the same league with AXE or some of the counter-espionage organizations in other countries that we have to contend with. Like the Ah Fu in Red China for instance, or the N.O.J. of South Africa.

To my mind, the FBI was an effective, dedicated group of amateurs.

Hawk read the thoughts in my expression and held up a palm. "Easy, Nick, easy. This is important. Very important, and the President asked for you himself."

I was dumbfounded.

Hawk continued. "He heard about you from the Haitian affair, I know, and probably from a couple of other assignments. Anyway, he asked for you specifically."

I rose to my feet and took a few quick turns up and down the short length of what served as my living room. Impressive. Few men in my business are personally selected at the Presidential level.

I turned to Hawk, trying not to show my prideful pleasure. "Okay. Would you fill in the details?"

Hawk sucked on his cigar, which had gone out, then looked at it in surprise. No cigar, of course, should dare go out when David Hawk was smoking it. He looked at it in disgust and scowled. When he was good and ready, he began explaining.

"As you probably know," he said, "the Mafia these days is no longer a ragtag collection of Sicilian hoods running bootleg whiskey and bankrolling floating crap games."

I nodded.

"In recent years—beginning, say, about twenty years ago—the Mafia began moving more and more into legitimate business. They did very well, naturally. They had the money, they had the organization, they had a ruthlessness that American business had never dreamed of before."

I shrugged. "So? This is all common knowledge."

Hawk ignored me. "Now, however, they're in trouble. They've expanded so far, and diversified so much, that they're losing their cohesiveness. More and more of their young men are going into legitimate enterprise, and the Mafia—or the Syndicate, as they call themselves now—is losing control over them. They still have the money, of course, but their organization is breaking down and they're in trouble."

"Trouble? The last report I read said organized crime was at its peak in America, that it had never done as well."

Hawk nodded. "Their income is up. Their influence is up. But their organization is breaking down. When you're speaking of organized crime now, you're not just talking about the Mafia. You're also talking about blacks, Puerto Ricans, Chicanos out west, and Cubans in Florida. Everybody is getting into the act.

"You see, we've been aware of this trend for quite a long time now, but so has the Mafia Commission." He permitted another pale smile to soften his weathered features. "You do know what the Commission is, I presume?"

I gritted my teeth. The Old Man can be so goddamned infuriating when he takes that patronizing air. "Of course I know!" I said, my irritation at his method of explaining this assignment obvious in my voice. I knew very well what the Commission was. Seven of the most powerful Mafia *capos* in the United States, each the head of one of the major families, named by their peers to serve as a governing board, the court of final appeal, Sicilian style. They didn't meet often, only when a major crisis threatened, but their decisions, carefully considered, absolutely pragmatic, were inviolable.

The Commission was one of the strongest ruling bodies in the world, when you took into consideration its effect on crime, violence and, perhaps most importantly, big business. I scanned my memory bank. Bits and pieces of information were beginning to click into place now.

I frowned in concentration, then recited in a monotone: "Government Security Information Bulletin Number Three-twenty-seven, June eleven, 1973. 'Latest information indicates the Syndicate Commission now comprises the following:

" 'Joseph Famligotti, sixty-five, Buffalo, New York.

" 'Frankie Carboni, sixty-seven, Detroit, Michigan.

" 'Mario Salerno, seventy-six, Miami, Florida.

" 'Gaetano Ruggiero, forty-three, New York, New York.

" 'Alfred Gigante, seventy-one, Phoenix, Arizona.

" 'Joseph Franzini, sixty-six, New York, New York.

" 'Anthony Musso, seventy-one, Little Rock, Arkansas.' "

Easy. I waved a casual hand in the air-conditioned atmosphere. "Shall I give you a breakdown on each one of them?"

Hawk glared at me. "That's enough, Carter," he snapped. "I know you have a photographic mind . . . and you know I won't tolerate even subliminal sarcasm."

"Yes, sir." I would only take that sort of thing from David Hawk.

In slight embarrassment, I moved over to the hi-fi set and took off the three jazz records that had played through. "I'm sorry. Please continue," I said, sitting down again in the captain's chair facing Hawk.

He picked up where he'd left off a few minutes before, prodding the air in front of me with his cigar for emphasis. "The point is, the Commission can see as well as we can that success is gradually modifying the Syndicate's traditional structure. Like any other group of old men, the Commission is trying to block change, trying to bring things back to the way they used to be."

"So what are they going to do?" I asked.

He shrugged. "They've already started. They're bringing in what amounts to a whole new army. They've been recruiting all over Sicily, young, tough banditos out of the hills, just like they were when they—or their fathers—began."

He paused, chewing on the end of the cigar. "If they succeed well enough, the country could be in for a wave of gang violence that would match what we went through in the early '20s and '30s. And this time it would have racial overtones. The Commission wants to run the blacks and Puerto Ricans out of their territories, and they're not going to go without a fight, you know that."

"No way. But how are the old Dons getting their new recruits into the country?" I asked. "Have we any idea?"

Hawk's face was impassive. "We know exactly—or rather, we know the mechanism if not the details."

"Just a minute." I got up and took both our glasses over to the plasticized little counter that served as both bar and dinner table in SAMOCO's executive officer quarters. I made him another Scotch and water, splashed some brandy and soda into mine along with another ice cube, then sat back down again.

"Okay."

"It's really well done," he said. "They siphon their recruits through Castellemare in Sicily, then take them by boat to the island of Nicosia—and you know how Nicosia is."

I knew. Nicosia is the sewer of the Mediterranean. Every bit of slime that oozes out of Europe or the Middle East eventually coagulates in Nicosia. In Nicosia, the prostitute is the sophisticate, and what the others do on lower social scales is indescribable. In Nicosia, smuggling is an honored profession, thievery an economic mainstay, and murder a pastime.

"From there," Hawk went on, "they're smuggled on to Beirut. In Beirut, they are given new identities, new passports, then sent on to the States."

That didn't seem too difficult, but I was sure I didn't have all the details. Details were not one of Hawk's strongpoints. "That shouldn't be too hard to stop, should it? Just order extra security checks and identification data on everyone entering the country with a Lebanese passport."

"It isn't as easy as that, Nick."

I knew it wouldn't be.

"All their passports are American. They're forged, we know that, but they are so good we can't tell the false ones from the ones the government issues."

I whistled. "Anyone who could do that could make a small fortune in his own right."

"Whoever is doing it, probably is," Hawk agreed. "But the Mafia has lots of small fortunes to put out for such services."

"You could still put out a stop order on everyone coming from Beirut. It shouldn't really take too much interrogation to determine that the guy on the passport really comes from Sicily instead of the Lower East Side of Manhattan."

Hawk shook his head patiently. "It's not that easy. They bring them in from all over Europe and the Middle East, not just Beirut. They start in Beirut, that's all. Once they have their new identity papers and passports, they're often flown to another city, then put on a plane for the States. Mostly, they've been coming in on return charter flights, which lack so much basic organization to begin with that they're hard to control.

"Usually they have a group of them aboard the big cruise ships when they return to the States, too," he added.

I took a long swallow of my brandy and soda and pondered the situation. "You must have an agent on the inside by this time."

"We've always had agents inside the Mafia, or—that is—the FBI has, but they're pretty hard to maintain. Either their cover gets blown somehow, or they have to blow it themselves in order to testify."

"But you do have someone in there now," I pressed.

"The FBI does, of course, but we have no one in this pipeline that's bringing in the new recruits. That's one of our prime concerns."

I could see the direction in which things were going now. "Then that's what you want me for? To get into the pipeline?" Hell, that shouldn't be too hard. It was a project that would take some thought, but certainly one that could be done easily enough.

"Well," Hawk was equivocating, "yes. I mean, basically that's it. You see," he continued slowly, "the original plan called for us to get a man into the pipeline, then expose it, break it up, whatever. And it had to be one of our men. You know the FBI is out of the question when we're dealing in a foreign country."

I nodded.

"It could have been the CIA, of course, but it's too tied up with that Argentina thing right now, and anyway, the President . . ."

I finished the sentence for him. "And anyway, the President isn't too happy with the CIA these days, particularly with Grefe."

Bob Grefe was the current CIA chief and his differences with the President had been in every Washington "insiders" column for a month.

"Quite right," Hawk said, looking grim. "So they decided it was a job for AXE."

"Okay." But that left a lot unsaid. Why me, for instance? There were lots of good men in AXE. "What else?"

"Well," he said. "This whole idea of AXE planting a man in the pipeline had to be brought to the President's attention, of course, since there's a State Department angle involved." Hawk paused, searching for the right words, I guessed. "He thought it was a great idea, but then he said as long as we were going to do that, we might as well carry it a step further right on through to the top."

Somehow, I didn't like the sound of that. "What does 'right on through to the top' mean?"

"It means you wipe out the Commission," Hawk stated bluntly.

I sat for a moment in stunned silence. "Now hold on a minute, sir! The government has been trying to get rid of the Commission since 1931, when they first found out it existed. Now you want me to do it?"

"Not me." Hawk looked smug. "The President."

I shrugged with a show of indifference which I didn't feel. "Well, then I guess I'll have to give it a try."

I looked at my watch. "I've got to make out my report on Raschid and the Dutchman," I said. "Then I guess I'd better catch a flight to Beirut, first thing in the morning."

One last night with Betty Emers, I thought. Betty with those exquisite breasts and her neat, businesslike approach to life.

Hawk stood up, also. He took an envelope out of his shirt pocket and handed it to me. "Here's your ticket to Beirut," he said. "It's the KLM flight out of Karachi. Arrives here at six-twenty-three this evening."

"This evening?"

"This evening. I want you on it." Surprisingly, he reached over and shook my hand. Then he turned and let himself out the door, leaving me standing in the middle of the room.

I drained my drink, set the glass down on the counter, and went into the bathroom to pick up my clothes from the floor and start putting my stuff together.

As I picked up my bush jacket, the aluminum container of heroin I had taken from Hamid Raschid's broiled carcass fell to the floor.

I picked up the tube and looked at it, pondering what to do with it. I'd thought of turning it in, but now I had another idea. I realized I was the only one in the world who knew I had it.

All I needed were a couple of cigars that came in that

type of container and it would be like playing the old three-shells-and-the-pea game at the carnival.

I smiled to myself and tucked the heroin away in my hip pocket.

Then I retrieved Wilhelmina from her spring holster on my dresser and began cleaning her meticulously, my mind racing.

CHAPTER 3

The flight to Beirut was uneventful. I spent the two hours trying to push thoughts of Betty Emers from my mind with attempts at mapping out a plan of action once I got to Lebanon.

In my business, of course, you can't really plan too far ahead. Nonetheless, a certain amount of direction is needed to get started. After that, it's more like Russian roulette.

The first thing I would need would be a new identity. Actually it shouldn't be too difficult. Charlie Harkins was in Beirut, or had been last time I had been there, and Charlie was a good, working penman, very good with passports, false bills of lading, that sort of thing.

And Charlie owed me a favor. I could have implicated him when I broke up that Palestinian bunch bent on overturning the Lebanese government, but I had deliberately omitted his name from the list I'd turned over to the authorities. He was small fry anyway, and I figured he might come in handy some day. Those type of people always do.

My second problem in Beirut was a bit more formidable. Somehow, I had to get myself into the Mafia pipeline.

The best way—I guessed the only way—would be to pose as an Italian. Well, between my naturally dark complexion and Charlie's penmanship, that could be arranged.

I fingered the metal tube of heroin alongside the two identical tubes containing expensive cigars. That heroin could be my entrée into the charmed circle.

My thoughts drifted back to Betty Emers and the muscle in my thigh jumped. I fell asleep, dreaming.

Even at nine o'clock at night, Beirut Airport was hot and dry.

The Government Business overlay on my passport drew a few raised eyebrows from the Lebanese customs personnel, but it got me through the long lines of white-robed Arabs and business-suited Europeans. Within minutes I was outside the terminal building and trying to cram my legs into the back seat of a tiny Fiat taxicab.

"The St. Georges Hotel," I ordered, "and for Chrissake, take it easy." I had been in Beirut before. The stretch of precipitous road that snakes down from the airport to the city edges along plummeting cliffs is one of the more hair-raising routes devised by man. The cab driver turned in his seat and flashed me a grin. He was wearing an open-necked, bright yellow sport shirt, but on his head was a *tarboosh,* the conical red fez of Egypt.

"Yes, sir," he laughed. "Yes, sir. We fly low and slow!"

"Just slow," I grumbled.

"Yes, sir!" he repeated, chuckling.

We catapulted out of the airport at top speed, tires

squealing, and made the turn onto the Beirut road on two
wheels. I sighed, sat back on the seat and forced my
shoulder muscles to relax. I closed my eyes and tried to
think of something else. It had been that kind of a day.

Beirut is an ancient Phoenician city dating back before
1500 B.C. According to legend it was the spot on which
St. George slew the dragon. Later, the city had been captured by the Crusaders under Baldwin, and still later by
Ibrahim Pasha, but it had withstood the siege guns of Sal-
adin and defied the British and French. Bouncing around
in the back seat of the hurtling Fiat as we plummeted
down the Beirut road, I wondered what it held for me.

The St. Georges Hotel rises tall and elegant on the
palm-fringed shore of the Mediterranean, oblivious to the
filth and incredible poverty of the Thieves' Quarter, only
a few blocks away.

I requested a southwest corner room above the sixth
floor, got it, and registered, surrendering my passport to
the unctious room clerk as is demanded by law in Beirut.
He assured me it would be returned within a few hours.
What he meant was, within a few hours after Beirut Security had checked it out. But that didn't bother me; I
wasn't an Israeli spy out to blow up a bunch of Arabs.

Actually, I was an American spy out to blow up a
bunch of Americans.

Once I had unpacked and checked the view of the
moonlit Mediterranean from my balcony, I called Charlie
Harkins and told him what I wanted.

He was hesitant. "Well, you know I'd like to help you,
Nick." There was a high nervous whine to his voice.
There always had been. Charlie was a nervous, whining
man. He went on: "It's just that . . . well . . . I'm sort of
out of that business now and . . ."

"Bull!"

"Well, yeah, I mean, no. I mean, well, you see . . ."

I didn't care what his problem was. I let the volume of my voice drop several decibels. "You owe me one, Charlie."

"Yeah, Nick, yeah." He paused. I could almost hear him looking nervously over his shoulder to see if anyone else were listening. "It's just that I'm supposed to be working exclusively for one outfit now and not for anyone else and . . ."

"Charlie!" I let my impatience and irritation show.

"Okay, Nick, okay. Just this one time, just for you. You know where I live?"

"Could I have called you up if I didn't know where you lived?"

"Oh, yeah, yeah. Okay. How about eleven o'clock then . . . and bring a picture of yourself with you."

I nodded into the phone. "Eleven o'clock." Hanging up, I lay back in the luxury of the white-slipped giant bed. Only hours before I had been worming my way up that giant sand dune on a death hunt for Hamid Raschid and the Dutchman. I liked this kind of assignment better, even if there wasn't a Betty Emers around.

I looked at my watch. Ten-thirty. Time to see Charlie. I rolled off the bed, made an instant decision that the lightweight tan suit I was wearing would do for the likes of Charlie Harkins, and was on my way. Once I finished with Charlie, I thought I might stop by the Black Cat Café or the Illustrious Arab. It had been a long time since I had had a taste of Beirut nightlife. But today had been a very long day. I hunched my shoulders forward, stretching the muscles. I just might go right to bed instead.

Charlie lived on Almendares Street, about six blocks from the hotel and just on the eastern edge of the Thieves Quarter. Number 173. I climbed three flights of the filthy, dimly lit staircase. It was dank, in the airless heat, with the stench of urine and rotting garbage.

At each landing, four once-green doors opened off a short hallway opposite a sagging wooden railing that jutted precariously over the stairwell. From behind the closed doors came muted shrieks, shouts, gales of laughter, furious obscenities in a dozen languages, blaring radios. On the second floor, a great crash splintered a faceless door just as I was passing by and four inches of axe blade protruded through the wooden paneling. Inside, a woman screamed, long and warbling, like an alley cat on the prowl.

I took the next flight of steps without pausing. I was in one of the biggest red-light districts in the world. Behind similar faceless doors in a thousand faceless tenements in the garbage-strewn streets of the Quarter, thousands upon thousands of whores vied with each other for the monetary rewards of satisfying the sexual needs of the dregs of humanity who had washed into the teeming slums of Beirut.

Beirut is at once the gem of the Mediterranean and the cesspool of the Mideast. Ahead of me a door flew open and a greasy fat man staggered out. He was stark naked except for a ludicrous *tarboosh* sitting tightly on his head. His face was twisted into an agony-ecstasy grimace, his eyes glazed with either pain or pleasure, I couldn't tell which. Behind him came a lithe jet-black girl, dressed only in hip-high leather boots, her heavy-lipped countenance a phlegmatic mask as she stalked relentlessly after the fat Arab. Twice she flicked her wrist and twice a three-lashed whip, tiny, dainty and excruciating, slicked out and around the Arab's larded thighs. A gasp of pain escaped him and six tiny rivulets of blood etched his shaking flesh.

The Arab staggered past me, oblivious to anything but his own torturous joy. The girl stalked behind him, poker-faced. She couldn't have been over 15 years old.

I told my stomach to forget it and went up the last flight of stairs. Here a single doorway blocked the staircase. I pushed the buzzer. Charlie Harkins had occupied the entire third floor for as long as I had known him. In the few seconds before he answered, a picture of the sprawling squalor of his loft-like apartment flashed through my mind: His brightly-lit bench, with its cameras, brushes, pens, and engraving equipment were always there like an island of calm among the dirty socks and underwear, some of which, I remembered, looked as if they had been used to wipe clean the exquisitely tooled little platen press in the corner.

This time, it took me a moment to recognize the little man who opened the door. Charlie had changed. Gone were the sunken cheeks, the three-day stubble of gray beard he had always seemed to maintain. Even the dead, hopeless look in his eyes was gone. Charlie Harkins now looked bright, wary perhaps, but no longer as terrified of life as he had been over the years I had known him.

He wore a lightweight plaid sports jacket, neatly pressed grey flannel trousers and brightly shined black shoes. This was not the Charlie Harkins I had known. I was impressed.

He ushered me in with a tentative handshake. At least *that* hadn't changed.

The apartment had, however. What had been a littered mess was now neat and clean. A fresh green rug covered the old scarred floorboards and the walls were painted a neat off-white. Inexpensive but obviously new furniture was placed strategically to break up the barnlike lines of the big room . . . a coffee table, several chairs, two couches, a long, low, rectangular platform bed in one corner.

What had once served haphazardly as Charlie's work corner was now partitioned off with louvered panels and, from the evidence escaping through the openings of the partitions, vividly lit.

I raised my eyebrows, looking around. "Looks like you've been doing pretty well, Charlie."

He smiled nervously. "Well ... uh ... business has been pretty good, Nick." His eyes brightened. "I've got a new assistant now and things have really been going all right . . ." His voice trailed off.

I grinned at him. "It would take more than a new assistant to do this to you, Charlie." I waved my hand at the new decor. "Off hand, I'd say that for once in your life you've found something steady."

He ducked his head. "Well . . ."

It wasn't common to find a forger with a steady business. That sort of work tends to go in sudden spurts and long stoppages. What it probably meant was that Charlie had somehow gotten into the counterfeit game. Personally, I didn't care what he was doing as long as I got what I came for.

He must have been reading my mind. "Uh ... I'm not so sure I can do this, Nick."

I gave him a friendly smile and sat down on one of the double-ended sofas that sat at right angles with its twin, making a false corner in the middle of the living room. "Sure you can, Charlie," I said easily.

Taking Wilhelmina out of her holster, I waved it carelessly in the air. "If you don't, I'll kill you." I wouldn't have of course. I don't go around killing people for something like that, particularly little people like Charlie Harkins. But then, Charlie didn't know that. All he knew was that I could kill people on occasion. The thought apparently occurred to him.

He thrust out a pleading palm. "Okay, Nick, okay. It's just that I'm not . . . well, anyway . . ."

"Okay." I reholstered Wilhelmina and leaned forward, my elbows on my knees. "I need a whole new identity, Charlie."

He nodded.

"When I leave here tonight, I'm going to be Nick Cartano, originally from Palermo, more recently from the French Foreign Legion. Leave me about a year or so between the Foreign Legion and now. I can fake that." The fewer actual facts people had to check back on, the better off I would be.

Harkins frowned and pulled at his chin. "That means a passport, discharge papers . . . what else?"

I ticked them off on my fingers. "I'll need personal letters from my family in Palermo, from a girl in Syracuse, a girl from St. Lo. I want a driver's permit from St. Lo, clothes from France, an old suitcase, and an old wallet."

Charlie looked distressed. "Gee, Nick, I can get that stuff all right, I guess, but it will take some time. I'm not supposed to being doing anything for anybody else now and I'll have to go slow and . . . uh . . ."

Again, I got the impression that Charlie was working steadily for someone else. But at the moment, I couldn't have cared less.

"I want it tonight, Charlie," I said.

He sighed in exasperation, started to say something, then thought the better of it and pursed his lips, thinking. "I can do the passport and the discharge papers, all right," he finally said. "There's enough demand for those that I've got forms on hand, but . . ."

"Get them," I interrupted.

He looked at me dismally for a moment, then shrugged his shoulders in resignation. "I'll try."

Some people just won't do anything unless you lean on them. I leaned on Charlie and about midnight that night I walked out of that plastic elegance into the fetid streets of the Quarter as Nick Cartano. A phone call to our embassy would take care of my old passport and the few belongings I had left in the Hotel St. Georges. From now until I finished this job, I was Nick Cartano, a footloose Sicilian with a cloudy past.

I whistled a light Italian tune as I went down the street.

I moved into the Hotel Roma and waited. If there was a stream of Sicilians pouring through Beirut on their way to America, they would be coming through the Roma. The Roma in Beirut is an irresistible attraction for Italians, as if the front desk were decorated with cloves of garlic. Actually, the way it smells, it could be.

For all my planning, however, I met Louie Lazaro by pure chance the very next day.

It was one of those flatly hot days you find so often along the coast of Lebanon. The scorching blast of the desert is there, sand dry and fiercely hot, but the cool blue of the Mediterranean lessens the impact.

On the sidewalk in front of me, hawk-visaged Bedouins, their black *abayas* trimmed with gold brocade, shouldered their way past sleek Levantine businessmen; flagrantly mustached merchants bustled by, talking excitedly in French; here and there appeared *tarbooshes*, their wearers sometimes in severely cut Western suits, sometimes in *galibeahs,* the ever present nightgown-like robe. On the curb, a legless beggar wallowed in the street's accumulated filth, wailing, *"Bahksheesh, bahksheesh,"* at each passer-by, his palms upturned in supplication and his rheumy eyes beseeching. In the street, a veiled old haridan perched high on a mangy camel that plodded along disconsolately, oblivious to the taxis dodging wildly through the narrow street, raucous horns honking in dissonance.

Across the street, two American girls were taking pictures of a Negebian family group as it paraded slowly down the street, the women balancing huge earthen jars on their heads, both men and women in the soft oranges and blues these gentle people so often affect in their robes and turbans. In the distance, where Almendares Street curves southward toward the St. Georges, the magnificent white sand beach was dotted with sunbathers. Like swirling ants on the blue glass sea, I could see two water skiers trailing their toy-like boats on invisible threads.

It happened suddenly: A taxi whipping blindly around the corner, the driver fighting the wheel as he swerved into the middle of the street to avoid the camel and then see-sawing back to miss an oncoming car. Tires screeching, the cab hurtled out of control in a careening side skid toward the beggar groveling on the curb.

Instinctively I moved, darting toward him in a headlong dive, half-shoving, half-throwing the Arab out of the path of the taxi and tumbling after him into the gutter as the cab smashed across the sidewalk and slammed against the stucco wall of the abutting building in a shrieking agony of rending metal.

For a moment, the world of Almendares Street was stunned into a wax museum tableau. Then a woman wailed, a long drawn-out moan that released her fear and seemed to echo the relief in the crowded street. I lay motionless for a moment, mentally counting my arms and legs. They all seemed to be there, though my forehead felt as if it had taken quite a thumping.

I got up slowly, testing all my working parts. No bones seemed to be broken, no joints sprained, so I moved over to peer through the front door window of the cab, jammed grotesquely against the unyielding stucco.

A multi-lingual babel swelled behind me as I ripped open the door and, as gently as I could, pulled the driver from behind the wheel. Miraculously, he seemed unscathed, only stunned. There was an ashen cast to his olive face as he leaned unsteadily against the wall, a tassled *tarboosh* improbably cocked over one eye, staring incomprehensively at the wreck of his livelihood.

Satisfied that he was in no immediate distress, I turned my attention to the beggar who lay writhing on his back in the gutter, too much in pain to help himself or, perhaps, too weak. God knows, he was as thin as any starving man I have ever seen. There was quite a lot of blood on his face, most of it from a deep gash high on his cheekbone, and he was moaning piteously. When he saw me leaning over him, however, he half-raised himself on one elbow and thrust out his other hand.

"*Bahksheesh, sadiki,*" he sobbed. "*Bahksheesh! Bahksheesh!*"

I turned away, revolted. In New Delhi and Bombay I have seen the living heaps of bones and bloated bellies that lie in the streets awaiting death by starvation, but even they have more human dignity than the beggars of Beirut.

I started to move away, but a hand on my arm detained me. It belonged to a short, pudgy little man with a cherubic face and eyes as black as his hair. He wore a black silk suit, a white shirt and white tie, incongruous in the heat of Beirut.

"*Momento,*" he said excitedly, his head bobbing up and down as if to lend emphasis. "*Momento, per favore.*"

Then he switched from Italian to French. "*Vous vous êtes fait du mal?*" His accent was atrocious.

"Je me suis blessé les genous, je crois," I answered,
flexing my knees carefully. I rubbed my head. *"Et
quelque chose bien solide m'a cogné la tête. Mais ce n'est
pas grave."*

He nodded, frowning but grinning at the same time. I
guessed that his comprehension wasn't much better than
his accent. He still had one hand on my arm. "Speak English?" he asked hopefully.

I nodded, amused.

"Great! Great!" He fairly bubbled with enthusiasm. "I
just wanted to say that was the bravest thing I've ever
seen. Fantastic! You moved so fast, so quick!" He was
quite carried away by the whole thing.

I laughed. "Just reflex action, I guess." And it had
been, of course.

"No!" he exclaimed. "It was courage. I mean, that was
real guts, man!" He pulled an expensive cigarette case
from his inside coat pocket, flipped it open and proferred
it to me.

I took a cigarette, and bent to take a light from his eager fingers. I didn't quite know what he was after, but he
was amusing.

"Those were the greatest reflexes I've ever seen." His
eyes shone with excitement. "Are you a fighter or something? Or an acrobat? A pilot?"

I had to laugh. "No, I . . ." Let's see. What the hell was
I? Right now, I was Nick Cartano, formerly of Palermo,
more recently of the Foreign Legion, currently . . . currently available.

"No, I'm none of those things," I said. I pushed
through the throng that had gathered around the wrecked
cab and the stunned driver and strode down the sidewalk.
The little man scurried to keep pace.

In mid-stride, he stuck out his hand. "I'm Louie La-zaro," he said. "What's your name?"

I shook his hand unenthusiastically, still walking. "Nick Cartano. How do you do."

"Cartano? Hey, man, are you Italian, too?"

I shook my head. "Siciliano."

"Hey, great! I'm Sicilian, too. Or . . . I mean, my par-ents were from Sicily. I'm really American."

That hadn't been too hard to figure out. Then a thought struck me and I suddenly became more amiable. It was true that not every American of Sicilian background in Beirut would have a connection with the Mafia pipeline I was looking for, but it was equally true that almost *any* Sicilian in Beirut *could* possibly aim me in the right direc-tion, either inadvertently—or intentionally. One Sicilian, it was reasonable to assume, could lead to another.

"No kidding!" I replied with my best look-at-me-I'm-a-delightful-guy smile. "I lived there a long time myself. New Orleans. Prescott, Arizona. Los Angeles. All over."

"Great! Great!"

This guy couldn't be for real.

"Jeez!" he said. "Two Sicilian-Americans in Beirut and we meet right in the middle of the street. It's a small god-damned world, you know?"

I nodded, grinning. "It sure is." I spotted the Mediter-ranean, the tiny little café on the corner of Almendares and Fuad, and gestured toward the beaded doorway. "What do you say we split a bottle of wine together?"

"Great!" he exclaimed. "In fact, I'll buy."

"Okay, man, you're on," I replied with make-believe enthusiasm.

CHAPTER 4

I'm not quite sure how we got to the subject, but we spent the next twenty minutes or so discussing Jerusalem. Louie had just returned from there, and I had once spent two weeks there, courtesy of Mr. Hawk's organization.

We toured the city conversationally, sightseeing in the Mosque of Omar and at the Wailing Wall, pausing at the Court of Pilate and Ruth's Well, following the stations of the cross up the Via Dolor and into the Church of the Holy Sepulchre, which still bears the carved initials of the Crusaders who built it in 1099. For all his effusiveness, Louie had a good grasp of history, a reasonably perceptive mind and a rather blasé attitude about the Mother Church. I was beginning to like him.

It took me a while to get the conversation going the way I wanted, but I finally managed it. "How long you going to be in Beirut, Louie?"

He laughed. Life, I was beginning to gather, was just one big lark to Louie. "I'm going back at the end of this week. Saturday, I guess. Sure had one hell of a time here, though."

"How long you been here?"

"Just three weeks. You know ... a little business, a little fun." He waved expansively. "Mostly fun."

If he didn't mind answering questions, I didn't mind asking them. "What kind of business?"

"Olive oil. Importing olive oil. Franzini Olive Oil. Ever hear of it?"

I shook my head. "Nope. I'm a brandy-and-soda man myself. Can't stand olive oil."

Louie laughed at my weak joke. He was the type who would always make a poor joke seem worth a laugh. Good for the ego.

I pulled a crumpled pack of Galoise from my shirt pocket and lit one while I happily set about making unexpected plans to become buddy-buddy with Louie Lazaro, the laughing boy of the Western world.

I knew Franzini Olive Oil, all right. Or at least I knew who Joseph Franzini was. Joseph "Popeye" Franzini. A lot of people knew who he was. These days he was Don Joseph, head of the second largest Mafia *famiglia* in New York.

Before Joseph Franzini had become Don Joseph, he had been "Popeye" throughout the underworld on the Eastern seaboard. The "Popeye" came from his very legitimate olive oil importing and marketing business. He was respected because of his ruthless integrity, his ritual adherence to the Mafia law of *omerta,* and his efficient business methods.

When he was thirty years old, Popeye had been stricken by some disease—I couldn't remember at the moment just what—that had forced him off the streets and into the administrative end of organized crime. There, his fine head for business proved invaluable and in a very short time he was able to achieve a position of real power in the gambling and loan-shark rackets. He and his two brothers built their organization carefully and solidly, and with business acumen. Now, he was Don Joseph, aging, querulous, jealous of the rights he had worked so hard to attain.

It was Popeye Franzini—Don Joseph Franzini—who was behind the move to reinforce the American organization with young blood from Sicily.

I had gone looking for some kind of an entré into Sicilian circles in Beirut, and it looked as if I had hit the jackpot. Certainly, Beirut was a logical port of call for an olive oil dealer. A good bit of the world's supply comes from Lebanon and its neighbors, Syria and Jordan.

But the presence of Louie Lazaro of Franzini Olive Oil at the same time the Mafia was funneling its new recruits through Beirut stretched the coincidence ratio too far.

I had another thought, too. Louie Lazaro might be more than just the bon vivant he appeared to be. Anyone who represented Popeye Franzini would be competent and tough, even if—to judge by the verve with which Louie was attacking the bottle—he tended to drink too much.

I tilted back on the heels of the little wire chair I was sitting on and tilted my glass at my new *amico*. "Hey, Louie! Let's have another *bottiglia di vino*."

He roared delightedly, slapping the table with a flat palm. "Why not, *compare!* Let's show these *Arabos* how they do it in the old country." The Columbia University class ring on his right hand belied his nostalgic reference as he signaled for the waiter.

Three days with Louie Lazaro can be exhausting. We saw a soccer game at the American University, spent a day visiting the old Roman ruins at Baalbeck; we drank too much at the Black Cat Café and the Illustrious Arab, and made it to just about every other bistro in the city.

During those three hectic days, I learned quite a lot about Louie. I'd thought he had Mafia written all over him, and when I found how deeply it was etched, all the bells started ringing. Louie Lazaro was in Beirut on Franzini Olive Oil business, all right—representing his uncle Popeye. When Louie dropped that bombshell over a fourth carafe of wine, I prodded my wine-fogged memory for information on him. Popeye Franzini had raised his brother's son, I remembered from a report I'd read at one time. Was this that nephew? He probably was, and his different last name, then, was most likely a minor cosmetic change. I didn't press him for a reason why he was called Lazaro and not Franzini, figuring that if it was relevant, I'd find out soon enough.

So I had virtually fallen into the hands of my ticket to Franzini's pipeline. My convivial, jesting companion, who gave a first impression of being a comic-opera Mafioso, must be pretty damned sharp under that talkative, wine-drinking mien. Either that, or Uncle Joseph had managed to shield his nephew from the ugly realities of organized crime, shuttling him safely into a legitimate end of the family operation.

Toward the middle of the afternoon on our third day of carousing, I made my move to determine the extent of Louie Lazaro's involvement in Uncle Joe's extra-legal affairs.

We were in the Red Fez, each table tucked into its own little walled niche, rather like stalls in a cow barn. Louie was sprawled loosely in his chair, one lock of black hair beginning to droop over his forehead. I sat erect but relaxed, my forearms on the little wooden table, drawing on what felt like my fortieth Galoise of the day.

"Hey, fella!" Louie burbled. "You're okay." He paused, examining his watch as people do when they're conscious of time, even when they're thinking in terms of days, weeks, or months instead of hours, minutes, or seconds. "We oughta get together back in the States. When you goin' back?"

I shrugged. "Know where I can get a good passport?" I asked casually.

He raised his eyebrows, but there was no surprise in his eyes. People with passport troubles were a way of life with Louie Lazaro. "Don't you have one?"

I sipped at my wine, frowning. "Sure. But . . ." Let him draw his own conclusions.

He smiled knowingly, waving his hand in dismissal. "But you do come from Palermo, right?"

"Right."

"And you grew up in New Orleans?"

"Right."

"Four years in the French Foreign Legion?"

"Right. What have you been doing, Louie? Taking notes?"

He grinned disarmingly. "Ah, you know. Just makin' sure I got things right."

"Right," I said. I knew where his questions were heading—at least I hoped I did—even if he didn't want to get to the point right away.

He picked up the cross-examination like any good prosecutor. "And the last couple years, you've been . . . uh . . . hanging round Beirut?"

"Right." I poured some more wine into each of our glasses.

"Well." He dragged it out, looking thoughtful. "I could

probably arrange it if you really want to get back to the States."

I glanced over my shoulder just for effect. "I sure as hell have to get out of here."

He nodded. "Maybe I can help you, but . . ."

"But what?"

"Well," he grinned that disarming grin again. "I don't really know much about you except you got a lot of guts."

I weighed the situation carefully. I didn't want to play my trump card too quickly. On the other hand, this could be my cracking point and I could always—if events warranted it—eliminate Louie.

I pulled the metal cigar tube out of my shirt pocket and dropped it carelessly on the table. It rolled over once and stopped. I stood up, and pushed my chair in. "I've got to go to the john, Louie." I patted him on the shoulder. "I'll be back."

I walked off, leaving the little tube worth, eventually, about $65,000 on the table.

I took my time, but when I got back Louie Lazaro was still there. So was the heroin.

I knew from the look on his face that I'd made the right move.

CHAPTER 5

At five o'clock that afternoon I met Louie in the lobby of my hotel. The silk suit was blue this time, almost an electric blue. The shirt and tie were fresh, but still white on white. His anxious-to-please smile was unchanged.

Outside on the street we hailed a cab. "The St. Georges," Louie told the driver, then settled back smugly in the seat.

It was only six blocks and we could have walked, but that wasn't what bothered me. What did was the fact that the St. Georges was the one place in Beirut where I was known as Nick Carter. The possibility that a room clerk or floor manager might greet me by name, however, was miniscule. Overfamiliarity is not a way of life in Beirut if you're obviously an American.

I needn't have worried. Even in my down-at-the-heels clothes, no one paid me the slightest bit of attention as Louie first made a quick call on the house phone in the lobby, then ushered me into the elevator, chattering nervously.

"This is a real good-looking lady, man! She's—she's really something else. But she's smart, too. Ooh mama! Is she smart!" He snapped his thumbnail on his front teeth. "But all you have to do is just answer her questions, you know? Just play it easy. You'll see."

"Sure, Louie," I reassured him. He'd been through the same routine a half-dozen times already.

A very tall, spare man with blue expressionless eyes opened the door of the eleventh-floor suite and gestured us in. He stood aside as Louie passed in, but when I followed he suddenly gripped the inside of my right elbow with viselike fingers and spun me around backward. A leg across the back of my knees threw me to the floor as he twisted, so that I hit the thick carpet on my face, my arm wrenched up high behind my shoulders and a bony knee pressed against the small of my back.

He was good. Not that good, however. I could have broken his kneecap with my heel when he made the first move, but that wasn't what I was there for. I lay there and let him remove Wilhelmina from her holster.

A hand made a cursory search of my body. Then the pressure on the small of my back eased. "All he had was this," he announced.

He was careless. Hugo still rested in the chamois sheath strapped to my forearm.

He nudged me with his toe and I got to my feet slowly. He'd pay for that later.

I brushed my hair back with one hand and took stock of the situation.

I was in the living room of a large suite and there were several doors leading off it. It was extravagantly decorated—to the point of opulence. The heavy, dark blue rug was complemented by gossamer-like draperies in robin'segg blue. Two Klees and a Modigliani were in perfect keeping with the clean-lined Danish Modern furniture.

Two couches were flanked by small onyx lamps and chrome-trimmed ashtrays. In front of each couch were heavy, low-slung coffee tables, large rectangles of gray marble sitting like pale islands in a dark blue sea.

Standing in front of the picture windows was an exquisite Chinese doll, one of the most beautiful women I had ever seen in my life. Her hair hung straight and black, almost waist length, framing delicate high-boned features. Almond eyes in an alabaster face regarded me somberly, a hint of skepticism tensing the full-lipped mouth.

I ruled my face expressionless while my mind clicked through its memory file. The ten days I had spent at AXE headquarters last year doing what we bitterly referred to as "homework" hadn't been wasted. Her picture on the dossier in File Room B had made me gasp the first time I had seen it. In the flesh, the impact was a hundredfold.

The woman in the high-necked gray silk evening gown before me was Su Lao Lin, next to Chu Ch'en the highest ranking intelligence agent the Red Chinese maintained in the Middle East. Chu Ch'en I had run up against before, both in Macao and Hong Kong; Su Lao Lin, I had only heard of.

What I'd heard was enough—ruthless, brilliant, cruel, fiery tempered but meticulous in her planning. She had been handling the pipeline funneling heroin into Saigon during the Vietnam war. Countless American G.I.s could lay the responsibility for their addiction at the exquisite feet of Su Lao Lin.

Now, obviously, she was in a different pipeline—funneling Mafia recruits into the States. This was no small-time operation. If Louie's uncle and the others on the Commission could afford Su Lao Lin, it would be a multi-million dollar investment, well worth it, perhaps, if they could gain—or regain—the great power they had wielded in the major cities in another time.

Looking at Su Lao Lin, my abdominal muscles tightened involuntarily. The gray silk, diaphanous in the light of the standing lamp behind her, only enhanced the perfection of that tiny body: the boldly full little breasts, the minute waist accentuated by the suppleness of neatly rounded hips, the legs surprisingly long for such a tiny person, the calves slim and lithe as you find so often among the Cantonese.

Sensuality crackled like lightning between the two of us. What Communist China's No. 2 agent in the Mideast was doing tied into the American-Sicilian Mafia was a mystery, but it wasn't the only reason I wanted to get my hands on her.

I let the lust show in my eyes and I could see her recognize it. But she didn't acknowledge it. She probably saw that same lust in the eyes of a half-dozen men every day of her life.

"You're Nick Cartano?" Her voice was soft but businesslike, the Oriental slur of the hard consonants only barely detectable.

"Yes," I said, running fingers through my disheveled hair. I glared at the tall hood who had rousted me as I came through the door. He stood just to my left, about a foot behind me. He held Wilhelmina in his right hand, pointing it toward the floor.

She gestured negligently, her deep red lacquered nails flashing in the lamplight. "Excuse the inconvenience, please, but Harold feels he must check everyone, particularly people with your . . ." She hesitated.

"My reputation?"

Annoyance clouded her eyes. "Your *lack* of reputation.

We haven't been able to find anyone who's ever heard of you, except Louie here."

I shrugged. "I guess that means I don't exist?"

She shifted slightly and the light from the window behind her poured between her legs, sharpening that exquisite silhouette. "It means either that you're a phony, or . . ."

That hesitation in mid-sentence seemed to be a habit.

"Or?"

". . . or you are very good indeed." A ghost of a smile flirted across the slightly parted lips and I smiled back. She *wanted* me to be "very good indeed." She wanted me, period. I could feel it. The feeling was mutual, but we still had to play the game for a while.

"In my business, we don't advertise."

"Of course, but in *my* business we usually can get a line on most people who are in . . . shall we say . . . allied lines?"

I fingered the shining cigar tube in my shirt pocket.

She nodded. "I know, Louie told me. But . . ."

I didn't blame her. She had a reputation for not making mistakes and my only tangible evidence of a "shady past" were the eight ounces of heroin in the tube. That and the fact that Louie had obviously been making a pitch for me. But Louie was the nephew of the man who was most likely bankrolling most of Su Lao Lin's operation. In the end, that had to be the deciding factor. She wouldn't want to displease Popeye Franzini's nephew.

She wouldn't want to displease herself, either. I stared at her insolently. Her eyes widened almost imperceptibly. She was getting the message, all right. I decided to take her off the hook.

I fished the pack of Galoise out of my pocket and tapped the open end against the side of my hand to bring out a cigarette. I tapped just a shade too hard and one popped out all the way and fell to the floor. I leaned over to pick it up.

Simultaneously, I bent my right knee and lashed straight back with my left leg. Behind me, Harold screamed as his kneecap crumbled under the hard rubber heel of my shoe, driven home with every ounce of power I could deliver.

I spun to my left, twisting into a sitting position. As Harold bent sharply forward, grasping for his shattered knee, I hooked two fingers of my right hand deep into the declivity under his chin, hooking them into the jawbone; I rolled back onto my shoulders, flipping him neatly.

It was like yanking a fish out of the water, throwing him forward and over me, so that he described a short arc in the air. Just before I lost my leverage, I jerked sharply downward and his face smashed into the floor with the full weight of his body behind it. You could almost hear the bones of his nose shatter.

Then he lay still. He was either dead from a broken neck or just unconscious from shock and the force of hitting the deck so hard.

I retrieved Wilhelmina and restored her to the shoulder holster where she belonged.

Only then did I smooth my hair back with one hand and look around.

Neither Louie nor the Chinese woman had moved, but the excitement had gotten to Su Lao Lin. I saw it in the slight flaring of her nostrils, the tautness of the vein running across the back of her hand, the flaring of intensity in her eyes. Some people are aroused to a high sexual fervor by physical violence. Su Lao Lin was breathing in short, quick gasps.

She motioned distastefully at what was left of Harold on the floor. "Remove him, please," she ordered Louie. She permitted herself a slight smile. "I think perhaps you're right, Louie. Your uncle could use a man like Mr. Cartano here, but I think you had better introduce him yourself. You had both better be ready to leave on the morning flight."

There was dismissal in her tone and Louie moved over to wrestle with Harold. Su Lao Lin turned to me. "Come into my office, please," she said coolly.

Her voice was controlled, but the overly modulated tone betrayed her. Excitement quivered on her lips. I wondered if Louie could sense it, too.

I followed her through the door into an efficiently equipped office—large modern desk with a businesslike swivel chair, a streamlined gray metal dictaphone, two straight metal chairs, a gray filing cabinet in one corner—a good place to work.

Su Lao Lin walked over to the desk, then turned and leaned back against the edge of it, facing me, her tiny fingers half-hooked over the edge of the desk top, her ankles crossed.

Lips parted over even teeth and a tiny tongue flicked out nervously, tempting.

I hooked the door with my foot and slammed it shut behind me.

Two long strides took me to her and a small groan escaped her lips as I crushed her to me, one hand under her chin, tilting it upward as my hungry mouth groped for hers. Her arms wound upward, curling around my neck as she thrust her body into mine.

I pinned her mouth with my tongue, probing, smashing. There was no subtlety. Su Lao Lin was incredibly small, but she was a wild woman, writhing, moaning, long nails ripping at my back, legs hooking around mine.

My fingers found the clasp on the high collar and unhooked it. The invisible zipper seemed to slide down of its own accord. I put both hands around her miniature waist and held her away from me, in midair. She broke reluctantly, fighting to keep her mouth clamped on mine.

I put her down on top of the desk. It was like handling delicate porcelain, but this porcelain could squirm.

I stepped back, pulling the gray silk dress away from her as I did. She sat still then, leaning back on her arms, her breasts heaving, the nipples outthrust, tiny feet flat on the desktop, her knees widespread. A rivulet of sweat ran down her belly.

She had been wearing nothing beneath the gray silk sheath. I stared, momentarily transfixed, savoring the alabaster beauty perched like a live *objet d'art* on the bare metal desktop. Slowly, unbidden, my fingers groped at my shirt buttons, fumbled at my shoes and socks, unhitched my belt.

I picked her up gently by the buttocks, balancing her like a cup on a saucer for a moment, and pulled her to me as I stood spraddle-legged before the desk. At the first penetration she gasped aloud, then scissored my waist with her legs so that she was riding on my hips.

Pushing against the desk for support, I leaned back with Su Lao Lin on top of me. The world exploded in a maelstrom of spinning sensation. Twisting, gyrating, we writhed around the sparsely furnished office in a feverishly hysterical dance, the two-backed beast upright, staggering into the furniture and against the wall. Finally, with a great shuddering spasm we crashed to the floor, driving, pounding, thrusting with every straining muscle until suddenly she screamed twice, two short, shrill yells, her back arched despite my weight pressing against her.

I pulled away and rolled over on my back on the floor, my chest heaving. With all the bedrooms in the world, I somehow had managed to end up on the floor of an office. I smiled and stretched. There are worse fates.

Then I became aware of a tiny hand on my hip. Delicate fingers traced a filigree pattern on the inside of my leg. Su Lao Lin, it was obvious, wasn't finished yet.

As a matter of fact, several hours passed before she was.

Then, once we had bathed, dressed and eaten the dinner I ordered sent up, she became all business.

"Let me see your passport.".

I handed it over. She studied it thoughtfully for a moment. "We'll have to get you a new one," she said. "An entirely different name, I think."

I shrugged, and had to smile inwardly. It looked as if my life as Nick Cartano was going to be very short indeed—not even a week.

"I want you out of here in the morning," she said.

"Why so fast? I kind of like it around here." That was true. It was also true that I wanted to find out as much as possible about the Beirut end of the operation before I left for the States.

She looked at me expressionlessly and I was forcefully reminded that this was Su Lao Lin, the Red Chinese agent who had sent so many American G.I.'s through hell along Heroin Highway, and no longer the delicate little wildcat on the office floor.

"Well? It has been an interesting evening, you'll admit."

"This is a business," she said coldly. "While you're around, I might forget that. I can't afford to . . ."

"So you want me out of here on the morning flight," I finished for her. "Okay. But can you fix up papers for me that fast?"

Charlie Harkins could, I knew. But I doubted if there were any more Charlies hanging around Beirut.

Su Lao Lin again permitted herself that ghost of a

smile. "Would I suggest it if I couldn't?" Her logic was hard to fault. "I want you to go now," she said.

I looked at my watch. "It's already ten o'clock."

"I know, but it's going to take some time . . . you must return here before you leave. Understand?" That ghost of a smile again. Su Lao Lin placed one tiny hand on my forearm and led me to the door.

I smiled at her. "You're the boss," I conceded. "Where do I go?"

"One-seven-three Almendares Street. It's over on the fringe of the Quarter. See a man named Charles Harkins. He'll take care of you. Just tell him I sent you. He's on the third floor." She patted my arm gently. It was probably the closest she would ever come to making an affectionate gesture.

I was cursing myself for a fool as I strode down the corridor and rang for the elevator. I should have known her penman was Charlie Harkins, which meant I had a problem. There was no way Charlie was going to fix me up with an entire new set of papers and not inform the Dragon Lady that she was playing around with AXE's No. 1 field agent.

There was one way, of course. I felt the reassuring weight of Wilhelmina against my chest as I stepped into the elevator. Poor old Charlie was going to get leaned on again, and this time it was going to have to be a pretty hard lean.

CHAPTER 6

Number 173 Almendares Street. The odors, noises and activities in the building were external. Charlie answered the doorbell almost before I took my finger off the buzzer. Whoever he had been expecting, however, it wasn't me.

"Nick. . . ! What are you doing here?"

It was a legitimate question. "Hi, Charlie," I said cheerfully as I pushed past him into the room. I sat down on one of the sofas in front of the coffee table, pulled a Galoise out of the half-crushed pack in my pocket and lit it with an ornate table lighter that looked as if it might have come from Hong Kong.

Charlie looked nervous as he closed the door, and after a moment of indecision, took a chair opposite me. "What's up, Nick?"

I grinned at him. "I've got another job for you, Charlie, and I want to talk to you a bit, too."

He assayed a small smile. It didn't come off too well. "I . . . uh . . . I can't talk much about things, Nick," he pleaded. "You know that."

He was right, of course. Half of Charlie's not inconsiderable value to the international underworld lay in his remarkable talents with a pen, a camera, a printing press, an airbrush, and an embossing kit. The other half lay in his absolute silence. If he ever talked about anything, he would be dead. Too many people in the Mideast would be too afraid that the next ones he talked about would be them. So silence was part of his stock in trade, and in my occasional brushes with Charlie I had never asked him to break it.

But life can be tough, I thought to myself. I had a moment's regret for what I was about to do, but I reminded myself that this was a presidential mission. The Charlie Harkinses of this world couldn't count for much.

"You should have told me you were working for the Dragon Lady, Charlie," I said conversationally.

He frowned as if he didn't know what the hell I was talking about. "What do you mean . . . uh, Dragon Lady?"

"Come on, Charlie. Su Lao Lin."

"Su Lao Lin? Uh . . . who's she?" Fright played with his eyeballs.

"How long have you been working for her?"

"Me? Work for who?"

I sighed. I didn't have all night to play games. "Charlie," I said with exasperation. "She sent me over here. I need a whole new set of papers. I'm leaving for the States in the morning."

He stared at me, comprehension finally dawning on him. I watched his eyes as he worked it out in his mind. He knew I was an AXE agent. If Su Lao Lin had sent me over to get new papers, it meant that I had worked myself into the pipeline somehow. And if I had worked myself into the pipeline, it meant that that pipeline wouldn't be operating much longer. He looked around the room as if seeing the freshly painted walls, the green rug and the nice furniture all disappearing before his eyes.

He had figured things out correctly.

"You're sure?" he asked.

"I'm sure, Charlie."

He sighed deeply. The fates were contriving against Charlie Harkins and he knew it. He had to let Su Lao Lin know that an AXE agent had broken through her security. But the AXE agent was right there in the room with him.

I didn't envy him.

Finally he made up his mind and sighed again. He reached for the telephone on the coffee table.

I leaned across the coffee table and slammed the palm of my hand hard across the bridge of his nose.

Tears welled in his eyes as he jerked backward. A trickle of blood ran from his left nostril. "I . . . have to call," he gasped. "I have to confirm that she sent you. If I didn't, she would know something was wrong. It's standard procedure."

He was undoubtedly right. There had to be some confirmation system, and the phone was as good a way as any. Now I had my own dilemma to contend with. If Charlie didn't call Su Lao Lin, she would know there was trouble somewhere. On the other hand, the last thing I wanted at that moment was Charlie on the phone with Su Lao Lin. I took Wilhelmina out of her holster with one hand and handed Charlie the telephone receiver with the other. "Here. Call her up, just as you would if I were one of your average Siciliano customers. Right?"

He nodded, frightened. "Sure, Nick."

I waved Wilhelmina under his nose. "I want you to

hold the phone so I can hear her, too. And I don't want you to say anything I wouldn't approve of. Understand?"

Harkins nodded bleakly. He dialed a number, then held the receiver halfway across the table and we both leaned forward so that our heads were almost touching.

The Dragon Lady's soft, aristocratic lisp came through the receiver. "Yes?"

Harkins cleared his throat. "Uh . . . Miss Lao?"

"Yes."

"Uh . . . This is Charlie Harkins. I got a guy up here who says you sent him."

"Describe him, please."

Inches away from me, Charlie rolled his eyes. "Well, he's about six feet four inches tall and has black hair combed straight back, kind of a square jaw and . . . uh . . . well, real broad shoulders."

I smiled at Charlie and waggled the tip of Wilhelmina at him.

"His name is Nick Cartano," he went on.

"Yes, I sent him over." I could hear her loud and clear. "We'll need everything—identity papers, passport, travel permit. He's leaving in the morning."

"Yes ma'am," Charlie replied dutifully.

"Charlie . . ." There was a pause on the other end of the line. "Charlie, have you ever heard of this Cartano? I wasn't able to get much of a line on him."

I nodded fiercely and tucked the muzzle of Wilhelmina under Charlie's chin to emphasize my point.

"Uh . . . sure, Miss Lao," he said. "I guess I've heard of him around town a little. He's been into a little bit of everything, I guess."

"Good." She sounded delighted.

Charlie stared uselessly at the telephone. He looked at me, dying to blurt out some kind of a warning.

I made a slight move with Wilhelmina.

"Goodbye, Miss Lao," he said. He hung up with a shaking hand, and I reholstered Wilhelmina.

He might have passed along some coded warning, or left out a confirmatory code, but I doubted it. The situation he was now in was too bizarre for his part of the operation to have ever been anticipated with such elaborate security.

For the second time since my arrival in Beirut, I went through the processing records routine with Charlie. He was good, but abysmally slow, and this time it took almost three hours.

I spent a good deal of time wondering how I was going to get rid of him. It was a problem. With Charlie alive, I'd never make it to the airport, let alone back to the States. Even if I left him bound and gagged, he would eventually get free and my goose would be cooked, no matter where I was.

The answer, obviously, was to kill him. But I couldn't do that. I've killed many times in my career, and Charlie was certainly no jewel of humanity. But I had killed as a final act of the hunt—men I'd been in combat with, or had stalked, or been stalked by. That's one thing. But Charlie was something else again.

There didn't seem to be any other way. Charlie had to go. On the other hand, if Harkins came up dead or missing just after fixing up my papers, the Dragon Lady was going to think it very strange indeed. It was a pretty little dilemma.

Charlie, however, solved it for me.

I was examining my new set of documents—for Nick Canzoneri this time. Charlie always liked to stay as close as possible to the real name. "Saves you from not responding sometimes when you should," he explained.

The papers all seemed in good order. There was a pass-port stating that Nick Canzoneri had been born in the lit-tle Calabresian village of Fuzzio, a workman's permit and a driver's license from Milano, a picture of an indistin-guishable young man and a girl holding hands in front of a Roman ruin and four whining letters from Nick Can-zoneri's mother back in Fuzzio.

Charlie had done a good job.

Then, as I was bending over the coffee table, looking at my new papers, he picked up the small lamp from the end table and smashed it across my head.

The force of the blow knocked me off the couch and onto the coffee table. I could feel it splinter beneath me as I crashed to the floor, the world a red haze of shrieking pain. I wasn't unconscious, thanks to the fact that the lamp had smashed. Schmitz's Law: The disintegration of a moving object dispels its force of impact in direct pro-portion to the speed of disintegration.

But I was hurting.

As I crashed to the floor, I instinctively sprung off the palms of my hands, throwing myself to one side in a roll. As I did, something else—probably the other lamp—smashed down next to my head, barely missing me.

I was on my hands and knees now, shaking my head like a wounded dog, trying to clear my brain. It felt as if a small bomb had exploded inside it.

I still couldn't see clearly. But I couldn't remain in one place. Charlie would be on the attack. From my hands and knees, I ducked my head into the crook of my arms and did a forward roll. My feet hit flat on the floor and I flipped upright.

I crashed against a wall. The jolt seemed to help. As I instinctively ducked just to keep moving, my vision began to clear. I could feel warm blood gushing down my face. I

leapt sideways. I didn't dare remain motionless until I
found my enemy. Any move I might make might take me
directly into him, but I couldn't stay still.

Then I found him.

He was coming around the corner of the couch after
me, one hand on the back of the couch, the other held out
from his side. It held a wicked looking curved knife. It
must have come from the decorative Arabic scabbard I
had seen hanging on the wall.

Charlie held the knife at waist height, pointed at my
belly. His feet were widespread for balance. He advanced
slowly.

My floundering gyrations may have saved my life, but
they had also left me crowded into a corner with the
couch along one wall and a heavy oaken table along the
other.

Charlie blocked my only route of escape.

I pressed against the wall as he took another step forward, only about four feet away now. His thin lips compressed tightly. The final lunge was coming.

I had no recourse. I snapped Wilhelmina into my hand
with an instinctive draw from the shoulder holster and
fired.

The bullet caught Charlie full in the throat and he
stood there a moment, brought up short by the shock of
the Luger. A look of puzzled surprise spread over his face
and he seemed to be looking at me as if I were a stranger.
Then his eyes glazed over blankly and the blood spurted
from the base of his throat. He fell over backward, the
knife still clutched in his hand.

I stepped gingerly over his body and went into the
bathroom to see if I could repair my face. If nothing else,
cold water would clear my head.

It took me a half-hour over the washbasin and another

twenty minutes over two steaming cups of black coffee that I made on Charlie's stove before I was ready to go. Then I picked up my Nick Canzoneri papers and headed back to the St. Georges. There were still the "special instructions" from Su Lao Lin before I could take off for the States.

And she had to be disposed of, too, before I left Beirut. I couldn't very well leave her there, pushing Siciliano hoods through the pipeline to the Mafia in New York. And since I was the last one she had sent to Charlie, his death wouldn't look so good for me.

I sighed as I rang for the elevator in the ornate St. Georges. I didn't want to kill the Dragon Lady any more than I had wanted to kill Charlie, but I had made one stop between his apartment in the Quarter and the hotel, and that stop would help me carry this part of the job out.

There was a softness in her eyes when Su Lao Lin opened the door for me, but it quickly turned to alarm as she looked at my damaged features. I had a strip of adhesive tape running across my temple over one eye were Harkins' lamp had cut a painful but actually superficial gouge, and that eye was swollen, probably discolored by now.

"Nick!" she cried. "What happened."

"It's okay," I reassured her, taking her in my arms. But she pulled back so that she could look up into my face. I remembered the fat Arab and the very young girl I had seen on my first trip up to Charlie's apartment. "I just got in between some Arab and his whore," I explained. "She hit me with a lamp instead of him."

She looked concerned. "You must take care of yourself, Nick . . . for me."

I shrugged. "I'm leaving for the States in the morning."

"I know, but I'll see you over there."

"Oh?" That was a jolt. I hadn't known she was planning to come to America.

Her smile was close to being demure. She put her head on my chest. "I just decided tonight, while you were gone. I'll be over there in a couple of weeks. Just to visit. I want to see Franzini anyway, and . . ." There was that mid-sentence pause again.

"And . . ." I prompted.

". . . and we can spend some more time together." Her arms tightened around my neck. "Would you like that? Would you like to make love to me in the United States?"

"I'd like to make love to you anywhere."

She snuggled closer. "Then what are you waiting for?" Somehow, that emerald green chiffon thing she had been wearing when she answered the door had disappeared. She wriggled her bare body against me.

I picked her up and headed for the bedroom. We had the better part of the night ahead of us and I wasn't going to spend it in an office.

I didn't tell her she would never get to the States, and the next morning I constantly had to remind myself of the American G.I.'s Su Lao Lin had destroyed with her drug network before I could bring myself to do what I had to do.

I kissed her softly on the lips when I left the next morning.

The plastique bomb I had attached to the underside of the bed wouldn't go off for another hour and a half, and I was sure she would sleep that long, probably longer if for some reason the acid took longer to eat through to the detonator.

I had picked up the bomb on my way to the St. Georges after I had left Harkins' place. If you ever need a plastique bomb in a foreign city, the place to get it is from the local C.I.A. agent-in-residence—and you can almost always find the C.I.A. agent-in-residence posing as the local Associated Press man. In Beirut it was Irving Fein, a little round man with horn rimmed glasses and a passion for drawing inside straights.

We had run into each other more than a few times around the Middle East, but he'd been reluctant to provide me with the explosive without knowing who I intended to blow up, and without checking with his boss first. He finally acceded when I convinced him it was a direct order from the White House.

It really wasn't, of course, and I might find myself in trouble over that later, but the way I figured, Su Lao Lin was an enemy agent and she had to be destroyed.

She was also very good in bed. Which was why I'd kissed her goodbye before I left.

CHAPTER 7

Louie met me at the Trans World Airlines gate at the airport an hour later. He had been talking to two swarthy men in inexpensive English-cut suits. They might have been olive oil merchants, but somehow I doubted it. As soon as Louie spotted me, he hurried over, hand outstretched.

"Good to see you, Nick! Good to see you!"

We shook hands heartily. Louie did everything heartily. Then he introduced me to the men he had been talking to, Gino Manitti and Franco Locallo. Manitti had a low, overhanging brow, a modern-day Neanderthal Man. Locallo was tall and spindly, and I caught a glimpse of a yellowish set of bad teeth through his tensely parted lips. Neither one spoke enough English to order a hot dog at Coney Island, but there was an animal hardness about their eyes, a tightness around the corners of the mouths that I'd seen before.

Musclemen. More grist for the Mafia mill.

Once on board the big airliner, I sat next to the winow, with Louie in the adjoining seat. The two newest recruits to the Franzini family sat directly behind us. During the entire flight from Beirut to New York, I never heard either one say a word.

It was more than I could say for Louie. He was bubbling from the moment we buckled our seat belts.

"Hey, Nick," he said with a leer. "What did you do last night after I left Su Lao Lin's? Man! That's some chick, huh?" He laughed like a little boy telling a dirty joke. "Did you have a good time with her, Nick?"

I looked at him coldly. "I had to go see a guy about my papers."

"Oh, yeah. I forgot. That would have been Charlie Harkins, I guess. He's a real good man. Best in the business, I guess."

Was, I thought to myself. "He did a good job for me," I said noncommittally.

Louie babbled on for a few more minutes about Charlie in particular and good penmen in general. He didn't tell me much I didn't already know, but he liked to talk. Then he changed the subject.

"Hey, Nick, you know you sure messed up that guy Harold in Su Lao Lin's apartment. Jeez! I never saw anyone move so fast!"

I smiled at my friend. I can be flattered, too. "I don't like getting rousted," I said toughly. "He shouldn't have done that."

"Yeah, yeah. I sure agree. But, damn, man, you almost killed the guy!"

"If you can't hit the ball, you shouldn't go to bat."

"Yeah, sure . . . man . . . The doctor at the hospital said that his kneecap was practically destroyed. Said he'll never walk again. He's got a spinal injury too. Might be paralyzed for life."

I nodded. Probably from that karate chop I'd give him across the back of the neck. It will do that sometimes when it doesn't kill outright.

I looked out the window at the disappearing Lebanese coastline, the sun glinting on the azure Mediterranean beneath us. I'd been on the job a little more than twenty-four hours and already two people were dead and one crippled for life.

At least, there should be two dead. I looked at my watch: ten-fifteen. The plastique bomb under Su Lao Lin's bed should have gone off a half-hour ago . . .

So far, I'd done my job. The mouth of the pipeline in Beirut was destroyed. But it was just a beginning. Next, I had to take on the Mafia on its home ground. I would be dealing with a solidly entrenched organization, a vast industry that spread across the country like an insidious disease.

I remembered a conversation I'd had with Jack Gourlay a few months before, just before I'd been given the assignment to run down the Dutchman and Hamid Raschid. We were drinking beer in The Sixish on Eighty-eighth Street and First Avenue in New York, and Jack had been talking about his favorite subject, the Syndicate. As a reporter for the *News*, he'd been covering Mafia stories for twenty years.

"It's hard to believe, Nick," he said. "I know one of those loan-sharking operations—the one run by the Ruggiero family—that's got more than eighty million dollars in outstanding loans on the street, and the interest on those loans is three percent a week. That's a hundred fifty-six percent interest a year on eighty million. Figure it out!

"But that's only seed money," he went on. "They're into everything."

"Like what?" I knew a lot about the Mafia, but you can always learn from the experts. In this case, Gourlay was the expert.

"Probably the biggest is trucking. Then there's the garment center. At least two-thirds of it is Mafia-controlled. They're in the meat packing business, they control most of the vending machines in town, private garbage collections, pizza parlors, bars, funeral homes, construction companies, real estate firms, caterers, jewelry businesses, beverage bottling concerns—you name it."

"Doesn't sound like they have much time for real crime."

"Don't kid yourself. They're big on hijacking, and everything they hijack can be funneled into their so-called legitimate outlets. The guy who expands his Seventh Avenue garment business is probably doing it on money that came from narcotics, the guy who opens a chain of delicatessens in Queens is probably doing it on money that came from pornography in Manhattan."

Gourlay had told me a bit about Popeye Franzini, too. He was sixty-seven years old, but far from retirement. According to Gourlay, he headed up a family of more than five hundred initiated members and some fourteen hundred "associate" members. "Of all the old 'Mustachio Petes,'" Gourlay said, "that old son of a bitch is by far the toughest. He's probably the best organized, too."

On the plane winging its way toward the States from Beirut, I looked at my seat companion, Franzini's nephew Louie. Out of the nineteen hundred gangsters who made up the Franzini family, he was the only one I could call a friend. And for anything besides a nonstop conversation, I doubted he'd be very useful if things got rough.

I looked out the window again and sighed. It wasn't the type of assignment I relished. I picked up a Richard Gallagher novel and began reading it, to get my mind off my immediate future.

After three hours I had finished it, we were still airborne, the immediate future still looked bleak, and Louie had started talking again. It was not a happy flight.

We were met at the airport by Larry Spelman, Franzini's personal bodyguard. Louie, I gathered, was held in fairly high regard by his uncle.

Spelman was at least an inch taller than my six-feet-four, but narrow and bony. He had a long, high-bridged nose and piercing, wide-set blue eyes. Gray speckled black in overlong sideburns, but he figured to be only about thirty-five years old. I knew him by reputation: hard as nails and fanatically loyal to Popeye Franzini.

He had a surprisingly booming laugh as he grabbed Louis by both shoulders in an affectionate grasp. "Good to see you, Louie! The Old Man sent me out here to meet you myself."

Louie introduced Manitti, Locallo and myself and we shook hands all round. Spelman stared at me curiously, the blue eyes unwavering. "Don't I know you from somewhere?"

He damned well might have. I could think of any of a dozen assignments on which I might have been pointed out to him. One of the factors in the success enjoyed by organized crime in this country has been its remarkable intelligence system. The underworld keeps as close tabs on government agents as the government does on underworld figures. I had never met Spelman personally, but it was quite possible he might recognize me.

Damn! I thought. I'm in the country five minutes and already I'm in trouble. But I played it nonchalant and hoped the deep tan I'd picked up in Saudi Arabia would throw him off a little. The adhesive tape across my forehead had to help, too.

I shrugged. "Ever been in New Orleans?"

"No. Not New Orleans." He shook his head fretfully. "You any relation to Tony?"

"Tony?"

"Tony Canzoneri, the fighter."

Goddamnit again! I'd forgotten my name was Canzoneri now, even after having heard Louie introduce me that way just a moment before. A few more lapses like that and I'd really be in trouble.

"He's my cousin," I said. "On my father's side."

"Great fighter!"

"Yeah." I had the feeling Larry Spelman was keeping the conversation going so he could study me longer. It was a funny game we were playing. He knew that I had just come from Madame Su Lao Lin in Beirut and that Canzoneri would not be my real name.

It wasn't a game I enjoyed. Sooner or later he was going to recall who I was and the whole charade would blow up. But there wasn't much I could do about it at the moment. "See you in a minute," I said. "I have to go to the john."

I took my bag with me, and in the privacy of a men's room stall, quickly transferred Wilhelmina and Hugo from the suitcase to their accustomed places: the shoulder holster for Wilhelmina, the spring-loaded chamois scabbard for Hugo. Security precautions being what they are these days in Lebanon, you don't board any airplanes carrying arms. On the other hand, a toilet kit lined with lead foil travels very nicely in a suitcase, looks perfectly innocuous and is impervious to baggage X-ray machines. Any customs inspector might decide to pick it up and look at it, of course, but life is full of chances, and for some reason I've never seen a customs inspector examine a toilet kit. They'll look in the toes of your slippers and smell your tobacco pouch to make sure it's not marijuana, but I've never seen one look in a toilet kit.

I left the men's room feeling a lot more secure.

The big Chrysler which Spelman drove back into the city was filled with Louie's chatter. For once, I appreciated his endless, laughing monologue. I hoped it would keep Spelman's mind off me.

It was just a little past 6:00 P.M. when the big blue car pulled up in front of a large, nondescript loft building on Prince Street, off lower Broadway. I was the last passenger to get out, and I looked up at the well-worn sign across the front of the building: *Franzini Olive Oil.*

Larry Spelman led us through the small-paned door and then down an open hall, passing a small office area where four women worked attentively over their typing desks wedged between a bank of gray filing cabinets and the wall. None of them looked up as we went past; in some businesses, it's best not to know who's coming and going around the office.

We came to a frosted glass door, neatly lettered with *Joseph Franzini.* As though we were all army draftees, newly arrived at boot camp, we filed in and lined our suitcases against one wall, then stood around looking self-conscious. Only Louie was immune to the regimental nuance the group had assumed; he vaulted over a small wooden railing and seemed to swarm all over a prim-looking secretary who had half-risen from her desk when she saw him enter.

"Louie!" she squealed. "When did you get back?"

He smothered her with kisses. "Just now, Philomina, just now. Hey! You're beautiful, honey, just beautiful!"

He was right. As she disengaged herself with some difficulty from his gorilla-like grasp, I could see that. Despite her appearance—rimless glasses, black hair pulled back in a tight bun, high-necked blouse—she was a true Italian beauty, tall, slim, but with exciting breasts, a remarkably small waist, and full, rounded hips. Her oval face, highlighted by huge brown eyes and a perky, defiant chin, was straight out of Sicily with its olive skin, sculptured features, and heavy, sensuous lips.

She smiled self-consciously in our direction as she stepped back of her desk, tugging her skirt straight. Momentarily, our eyes met across the room. Met and held, then she was busy sitting down again and the moment was gone.

Spelman had gone on by the desk and disappeared into an open office door behind and to the right of Philomina's desk. Louie perched on the corner of the secretary's desk, chatting with her in low tones. The rest of us found seats on the brightly colored plastic chairs just inside the door.

Larry Spelman reappeared, pushing a chrome wheelchair in which sat a huge old man. He was gross, filling the oversized wheelchair and spilling over the sides. He had to weigh three hundred pounds, perhaps more. Out of the mound of fat that formed his face glared baleful black eyes ringed strangely by dark circles, a classic example of the moon-face syndrome usually associated with cortisone treatment.

Just then I remembered something I had read a long time ago: Joseph Franzini was a multiple sclerosis victim. He'd been in that wheelchair for thirty-seven years— shrewd, defiant, ruthless, brilliant, powerful, and crippled by a strange neurological disease that strikes the central nervous system. It distorts or disrupts the motor impulses so that the victim can suffer loss of vision, lack of coordination, paralysis of the limbs, dysfunction of the bowels and bladder, and other problems. Multiple sclerosis doesn't kill, it just tortures.

There's no cure for MS, I knew, no preventive, not even any really effective treatment. Like most multiple sclerosis patients, Franzini had been struck down by the disease when he was young, at the age of thirty.

Looking at him, I wondered how he had done it. Except for a few short periods of spontaneous remission, Franzini had been confined to that wheelchair ever since, growing fat and bulbous from lack of exercise and his fondness for gorging himself on Italian pasta. Yet, he headed one of the most powerful Mafia families in the world with a business acumen and a reputation in underworld circles second only to Gaetano Ruggiero.

This was the man I had come to New York to work for, and to destroy if I could.

"Louie!" He barked, his voice raspy but surprisingly loud. "It's good to have you back." He glared malevolently around at the rest of us. "Who are these people?"

Louie hastened to make introductions. He gestured. "This is Gino Manitti."

"*Bon giorno,* Don Joseph." The Neanderthal man half bowed toward the crippled giant.

"*'Giorno.*" Franzini looked at Franco Locallo.

There was a quaver of fear in Locallo's voice. "Franco Locallo," he said. Then his face brightened. "From Castellemare," he added.

Franzini grunted and turned to me. I met his gaze steadily, but it wasn't easy. Hatred burned in those black eyes, but I'd seen hatred before. This was different.

Popeye Franzini hated with a fervor I had never encountered before.

Suddenly, I understood. Franzini's hatred was so malevolent because it wasn't directed at one man, or group of men, or at a country or an idea. Franzini hated himself. He hated his diseased body and because he hated himself he hated the God he had created in his own image.

Louie's voice cut across my thoughts. "This is Nick Canzoneri, Uncle Joe. He's my friend. I met him in Beirut."

I nodded toward the old man, not quite a bow.

He cocked one white eyebrow, or tried to. The result was more of a maniacal grimace as one side of his mouth gaped open and his head tilted to one side with the effort. "A friend?" he rasped. "You weren't sent over to make friends. Ha!"

Louie hastened to reassure him. "He's one of us, too, Uncle Joe. Wait till I tell you what he did one day."

It seemed strange to hear a grown man calling another one "Uncle Joe" but I guess it was all part of Louie's somewhat juvenile approach to life. And as for what he could tell about what I had done one day, he didn't know the half of it.

I smiled at Franzini as sincerely as I could, but I really couldn't think of anything to say so I just shrugged. It's a marvelous Italian way out of any situation.

The old man stared back steadily for a moment and then with a quick flick of his hands, half-turned the wheelchair so that he faced Louie. It was a remarkable move for a man who a moment before had had a difficult time cocking one eyebrow.

"Book these guys into Manny's," he ordered. "Give them tomorrow off, then tell them to report to Ricco." He looked over his shoulder at us. "Goddamn!" he said.

"They don't even speak English, I bet."

He glared up at Louie. "We got a party at Tony's Gardens tomorrow night. It's your cousin Philomina's birthday. You be there."

Louie grinned happily. "Sure, Uncle Joe."

His cousin Philomina blushed prettily.

The old man spun his wheelchair deftly and headed back into his office under his own power. Spelman looked me over coolly one more time, then followed his boss. If he'd ever known who I was, one of these days he was going to remember.

As Manitti, Locallo, and I followed Louie out of the office and down the hall, I had a very uneasy feeling about Larry Spelman.

CHAPTER 8

Manny's was the Chalfont Plaza, one of the grand old hotels on the east side of midtown Manhattan. The Chalfont Plaza had had more than one member of European royalty as a guest during its long history. It is still one of the standard stops for out-of-town businessmen visiting New York, and the Skycloud Room on the roof is a regular watering hole for the jet set.

Years ago, a group of prominent businessmen had bought the Chalfont Plaza from its original owners as a business investment, then later sold to Emmanual Perrini, a young, ambitious businessman with a lot of ready capital.

The sign on the front still says Chalfont Plaza, but the Mafia, to its eternal ego, refers to it as Manny's.

"Want to stop and have a drink, Nick?" Louie asked just before I stepped into the elevator after registering.

"No thanks, Louie," I groaned. "I'm exhausted."

"Okay," he agreed cheerily. "I'll call you tomorrow afternoon and let you know what's going on."

87

"Great." I mustered up one final friendly grin and waved goodbye as the elevator door closed. Exhausted? It wasn't just "jet lag" that made me forget to tuck Wilhelmina under my pillow before I went to sleep. Instead, I dropped her in her holster on top the heap of clothes I had left lying on the floor when I undressed.

When I woke up she was just four inches from my mouth and pointed directly at my left eye.

"Don't move, you son of a bitch, or I'll kill you."

I believed him. I lay perfectly still, trying to adjust my eyes to the momentarily blinding light from the bed-table lamp. Wilhelmina is only 9mm, but at that moment I felt as if I were staring down the muzzle of a sixteen-inch naval rifle.

I followed my line of sight up Wilhelmina's barrel to the hand that was holding her, then on up a long arm until I came to a face. Predictably, it was a familiar one: Larry Spelman.

My eyes burned from fatigue and as I came more fully awake I could feel the aches in my body. I had no idea how long I had been asleep. It felt like about thirty seconds.

Spelman jerked his hand and the steel-plated grip of my own pistol slammed against the side of my face. Pain welled up my jawbone. I managed to keep from crying out.

Spelman smirked and pulled back, still keeping the gun trained on me. He stood up, groped behind him with one hand for the nearby chair, and pulled it to him without ever taking his eyes off me.

He sat back in the chair and gestured with Wilhelmina. "Sit up."

Raising myself up cautiously, I tucked two pillows behind me. Nice and comfortable, except for that damned pistol. I glanced at my watch on the bed table. Three o'clock, and since no light showed through the blinds it had to be three o'clock in the morning. I had been asleep about four hours.

I looked at Spelman questioningly and as I became more awake decided he must be drunk. There was a strange look about his eyes; they didn't seem to be focusing properly. Then I saw that the pupils were contracted. He wasn't drunk, he was riding high on junk!

My jaw throbbed with pain.

"Think you're a pretty smart son of a bitch, don't you Carter?"

I winced mentally. He'd blown my cover, all right. I wondered if he had told anyone else yet. Not that it made a lot of difference. The way things looked at the moment, he would have all the time in the world to tell whoever he wanted.

"I don't feel very smart right now," I admitted.

He permitted himself a slight smile. "I finally remembered, about an hour ago. Nick Carter. You work for AXE."

Damn heroin! It will sometimes do that: trigger a long-forgotten memory. I'd seen it happen before.

"It was about four years ago," he went on. "Tom Murphy pointed you out to me down in Florida."

"Nice company you keep," I sneered. Beneath his façade of being a distinguished lawyer, the dapper gray-haired Murphy was one of the country's most successful purveyors of pornography. And in Murphy's case, it wasn't just a matter of sex and skin; he dealt in real filth.

Spelman jerked the pistol at me threateningly. "Who else is in this with you?"

I shook my head. "If you know I'm Nick Carter, you know I usually work alone."

"Not this time. As soon as I remembered who you

were, I called Beirut. Su Lao Lin is dead. Charlie Harkins is dead. Harold is in the hospital."

"So?" At least *that* part of my plan had worked.

Spelman smirked. "So you couldn't be working alone this time. That Chinese gal was killed almost an hour and a half after your flight took off."

"Oh?" I caught myself. It occurred to me that if Spelman thought I had other people working with me, it could buy me some time. I might even be able to implicate some of the legitimate members of Franzini's family. They might prove it a hoax soon enough, but it would cause some consternation at least.

I put that last thought out of my mind. My first job was not to cause consternation. It was to get the hell out of here alive. Right now, the odds didn't look too good.

"If I did have anyone working with me," I fenced, "why do you think I'd tell you?"

The muzzle of the Luger described a small circle in the air. "Popeye Franzini is gonna want the whole story," he said. Another little circle in the air. "And when I go tell him, I'm gonna give him every little bit of it."

Another point in my favor! Spelman hadn't told anyone yet. If I could just get rid of him before he got rid of me, things might start looking up. Starting from an unarmed semi-prone position on a soft bed was not my idea of a good start, but I was going to have to do something.

I had to get him close enough to make a grab at him and the only way I would be able to do that would be if I could provoke him into attacking me. The idea of deliberately provoking an attack from an armed, flying heroin addict wasn't the happiest one I had ever had. My chances were extremely slim. On the other hand, I didn't see any alternative.

"You're an ass, Spelman," I said.

He jerked the gun at me. It seemed to be his favorite gesture.

"Start talking, jerk, or you're going to die."

"Shove it!" I exploded. "You can't kill me until you know who I'm working with. You know that. Popeye wouldn't like that, Larry. Use your head—if you've got one with that snootful of horse running through your veins."

He thought about that one for a moment. Under normal circumstances, I think Larry Spelman was a reasonably bright man. Walking on a cloud of heroin, he was having trouble shifting the direction of his thoughts.

I kept talking. The more I talked, the longer I would live. "How did a nice Jewish boy like you get in the Mafia, Larry?"

He ignored me.

I tried another gambit. "Does your mother know she raised a heroin addict, Larry? She must be proud of herself. How many other mothers can say their sons turned out to be dope addicts who spend most of their lives pushing around a fat old man in a wheelchair? I'll bet she talks about you all the time, you know: 'My son the doctor,' 'My son the lawyer,' then your old lady pops up with 'My son the addict' . . ."

It was childish and it was hardly throwing him into an insane rage. But it did annoy him, if only because my voice was interrupting his junk-shrouded thinking.

"Shut up!" he ordered calmly enough. He took a half step out of the chair he was sitting on and almost casually smashed at me with the side of the Luger.

But this time I was ready.

I twisted my head to the right to avoid the blow and on the same instant flicked my left hand upward and outward, catching his wrist with a jarring karate chop that should have caused him to drop the gun, but didn't.

I rolled left on the bed, catching his wrist in my grip and pressing it palm-up against the white sheets, then lowering my shoulder over my upper arm to apply maximum pressure. His other arm circled my waist, trying to pull me back off the pinned hand.

He had my right arm immobilized against my own body. I made a quick, convulsive move, arching my back and getting one knee underneath me for leverage, and was able to free my arm. Now I had both hands free to work on his gun hand, the left one pressing his wrist flat in the tightest grip I could manage, the right one clawing at his fingers, trying to bend them back away from the gun.

I pried one finger loose and began bending it back slowly, inexorably. His fingers were fantastically strong. The pressure around my waist suddenly eased. Then his free hand snaked over my shoulder, and long bony fingers clawed at my face, hooking under my jawbone and yanking my head back, trying to break my neck.

We struggled silently, grunting with the effort. I worked on that gun finger, striving for leverage, while at the same time using every bit of my will power and muscles to keep my head down.

I gained an eighth of an inch with the finger, but at the same time I could feel my head being forced back. Spelman's fingers dug deep into my throat under my jaw, pressing my mouth grotesquely out of shape, his palm flattening my nose. In a moment, with the carotid artery cut off, I would lose consciousness.

A pink haze clouded my eyes and white streaks of pain flashed through my brain.

I opened my mouth and bit down hard on one of Spelman's fingers, feeling my teeth slicing into it like it was a

piece of barbecued rib. Hot blood welled into my mouth
as my teeth ground into his knuckle, seeking the joint's
weakness, then slashing through the tendons, crushing the
delicate bone.

He screamed and jerked his hand free, but my head
went with it, cocked into his finger by my teeth. I ripped
at it savagely, like a dog with a bone, feeling the blood
smear my lips and face. At the same time I increased the
pressure on his gun hand. His finger was bending now,
and I only had to snap it backward.

But my aching jaws were weakening and I started losing my grip on his finger. With a sudden wrench, he tore
free, but simultaneously, the fingers of his other hand
loosened their grip on Wilhelmina and the Luger fell to
the floor next to the bed.

Locked in each other's arms, we writhed on the bed in
straining agony. His fingernails sought my eyeballs but I
buried my head in his shoulder for protection and grabbed
for his groin. He twisted his hips to protect himself and
we rolled off the bed, onto the floor.

Something sharp and unyielding jammed into the side
of my head and I realized that I had hit the corner of the
bedtable. Now Spelman was on top, his sharp-featured
face inches from mine, his teeth bared in a maniacal grin.
One fist slammed into the side of my face, while the other
hand pressed against my throat in a choke hold, weakened
by his savaged finger.

I tucked my chin into my neck the best I could and
stabbed at his eyes with extended fingers, but he twisted
his head at the last minute to protect them, shutting them
tightly.

I grasped one big ear and jerked savagely, twisting. His
head snapped back around and I slammed the palm of my
hand into his beaky nose. I could feel the cartilage snap

loose under the force of the blow, and blood spurted out over my face, blinding me.

Spelman let out an agonized cry as I pulled loose from his grasp and rolled free. For a moment we faced each other on all fours, panting, gasping for breath, blood-smeared, two wounded animals in a confrontation.

Then I spotted Wilhelmina off to the side and near the bed table. From my hands and knees I went into a head-long dive, sliding forward on my stomach as I hit the floor, arms outstretched, fingers grasping for the gun. My fingernail scratched against the butt of the pistol and I lunged again. I felt a great exultation as my palm came flat down on the grip and my fingers circled it familiarly.

I had the gun, but like some big bony cat, Spelman was on top of me, his big hand pinning my outstretched arm, his other fist slamming like a piston into my ribs. I twisted onto my back, rolling my shoulder from left to right and pulling up my knees so that my legs were doubled against my chest.

Then I shoved violently outward with my feet, like an uncoiling spring. One foot caught Spelman in the stomach, the other in the chest, and he flew backward, breaking his grip on my wrist. He landed on his butt, the momentum carrying him over on his back. Then he rolled to the right, twisting his head down and under and came up on all fours, facing me.

He shifted to his knees, hands raised, slightly cupped, ready to attack. His face was a mess of blood from his broken nose. But single-minded bestiality glared from the pale blue eyes.

I shot him full in the face, at a range of about eight inches. His features seemed to collapse inward but he remained upright on his knees, his body swaying.

He was already dead but instinctively my finger moved

twice more on the trigger, pouring two more bullets into that battered face.

Then the body toppled forward and lay inert on the carpet before me, one lifeless arm flopping across my leg. I stayed where I was, gasping for breath, my chest heaving. The side of my head throbbed from the blow by the gun butt and it felt as if at least two or three ribs had been cracked. It was five minutes before I could finally stagger to my feet, and then I had to hold onto the bed table to keep from falling.

At first, I was afraid the sound of three shots would bring someone running, but in my befogged state I couldn't think of what I could do about it if anyone did, so I just stood there stupidly, trying to put my battered senses back together. In any other city in the world, the police would have been knocking on my door within minutes. I had forgotten I was in New York, where few cared and where no one got involved if he could help it.

At last I stepped over Spelman's body and staggered into the bathroom. Ten minutes in a steaming hot shower followed by a couple of minutes of biting cold did wonders for my bruised body and helped clear my mind.

From what Spelman had said, I was pretty sure he hadn't gone to anyone else with his information, once he had figured out who I was. I tracked back in my head. He had said, specifically in fact, something about *"when* Popeye Franzini finds out." Good enough. I was clear on that score, then, at least for the moment. Or at least I could hope I was.

I still faced a problem right at the moment. Being found in the same room with the battered corpse of Larry Spelman was entirely out of the question. There was no way such a situation could be an asset in my relations with the Franzini family. And I certainly didn't want any interference from the police. I'd have to get rid of him.

And I'd have to get rid of him in a way that he wouldn't be found for a while.

The Franzinis would be upset about Larry Spelman's absence, they would be in a rage if he turned up dead. And a rage can start people thinking: I'd showed up in Beirut one day, and four days later the Mafia's best pen-man in the Middle East was dead, along with their borrowed Chinese agent. Then, less than twenty-four hours after my arrival in New York, one of Franzini's top lieutenants was killed. It was a trend I didn't want the Franzinis to ponder. Larry Spelman couldn't be found just yet.

I thought about it while I dressed. What do you do with six feet five inches of dead and battered gangster? I couldn't exactly take him down to the lobby and hail a cab.

In my head, I ran through what I knew about the hotel, from the time I had come in the lobby with Louie, Manitti and Locallo, until the moment I had awakened with Wilhelmina's muzzle staring at me. There wasn't much, just a vague impression of heavy red carpets, gilt-framed mirrors, red-jacketed bellhops pushing buttons on self-service elevators, antiseptic hallways, a laundry room a few doors from my room.

Nothing much helped. I looked around my room. I had slept in it for several hours, almost died in it, in fact, but I hadn't really looked at it. It was pretty standard, a little mussed up at the moment, but standard. Standard! That was the key! Virtually every New York hotel room has a not-too-evident connecting door leading to the room next to it. The door was always securely locked, and they never gave you the key unless you had ordered connecting rooms. Nonetheless, that door was always or almost always, there.

Once I had thought of it, it was right there staring me in the face. The door next to the closet, of course. It just blended into the woodwork so nicely that you never really noticed it. I tried the handle perfunctorily, but of course it was locked.

That was no problem. I turned the lights all out in my room and put my eye to the crack between the floor and the bottom edge of the door. There was no light coming from the other side. That meant it was either empty or the occupant was asleep. At that hour, probably asleep, but it was worth checking.

My room was 634. I dialed 636 and held my breath. I was in luck. I let it ring ten times and then hung up. I turned the lights back on and selected two steel picks from the set of six which I always carry in my toilet kit. After another moment, the connecting door was unlocked.

Opening it, I moved quickly to the other wall and turned on the light; it was unoccupied.

Back in my room, I stripped Spelman's body and neatly folded his clothes, putting them in the bottom of my own suitcase. Then I dragged him into the neighboring room. Completely naked, his face a gory mess, he would not be immediately identifiable. And, as far as I could remember, he had never been arrested, so his prints were not on file, and his identification would be even further delayed.

I left Spelman's body inside the shower, with the frosted glass doors shut, and returned to my room to dress.

Downstairs at the front desk, I interrupted the young, red-jacketed clerk. He didn't like being taken away from his paperwork, but he tried not to show it too much. "Yes, sir?"

"I'm in room six-thirty-four, and if six thirty-six, next

to me is empty, I'd like to take it for a friend of mine. She's . . . uh . . . he's coming in later."

He grinned at me knowingly. "Sure thing, sir. Just register here for your friend." He spun the register pad at me.

Smart ass kid! I signed Irving Fein's name and an address I made up, and paid twenty-three dollars for the first night's rent.

Then I took the key and went back upstairs. I went into 636, took the "Do Not Disturb" sign, and hung it outside the door. I figured that three or four days could pass with that sign on the door before anyone made more than a cursory check.

I went back to my own room and looked at my watch. Four A.M. It had been just an hour since Spelman woke me up. I yawned and stretched. Then I took off my clothes again and hung them neatly over one of the chairs. This time, I made sure that Wilhelmina was tucked under my pillow before I climbed into bed.

Then I turned out the light. There wasn't much else to do in New York at four o'clock in the morning.

I fell asleep almost instantly.

CHAPTER 9

The next morning I checked out of "Manny's place" by nine o'clock. Spelman's clothes were packed along with mine in the suitcase, along with one of the sheets and a pillowcase, which had been smeared with blood.

From the Chalfont Plaza, I grabbed a cab heading downtown on Lexington and went to the Chelsea Hotel on Twenty-third Street just off Seventh Avenue. It's kind of a beat up old hotel these days and attracts a lot of odd characters. It had its days of glory, however. Dylan Thomas stayed there, and Arthur Miller and Jeff Berryman. My main reason for moving in there was far from literary nostalgia: Larry Spelman's body wasn't next door.

The first thing I did was to send out for some brown wrapping paper and a ball of twine. Then I carefully wrapped up Spelman's clothes, the sheet and the pillowcase, and took the package over to the post office.

I mailed the package to Popeye Franzini. The return address read "Gaetano Ruggiero, 157 Thompson Street, New York, N.Y. 10011." The longer Spelman's body remained undiscovered the better, but once it was found, I wanted suspicion directed away from me. I didn't know of any specific bad blood between the Ruggieros and Franzinis at the moment, but once that package arrived, there would be.

The current postal system is such that I could depend—with reasonable assurance—on the fact that a third-class package mailed from Twenty-third Street to Prince Street, a distance of about thirty blocks, would take at least a week.

I went into the Angry Squire, a pleasant little bar on Seventh Avenue around the corner from the hotel, and had a leisurely lunch washed down with two mugs of that good Watney's ale. Then I called Louie at his Village apartment.

Louie was ecstatic, as usual. "Hey, Nick! What's up, man? I tried to call you up at Manny's Place, but they said you'd checked out."

"Yeah. Too plastic for me. I moved down to the Chelsea."

"Great! Great! I know the place. Hey, look, Nick. Uncle Joe wants to see us this afternoon. Okay with you?"

I wondered if I had much of a choice. "Sure, why not."

"Okay, then. About two o'clock. At Uncle Joe's office."

"Okay," I reassured him. "I'll see you then."

It was a pleasant day and I walked, taking my time. I hadn't really seen much of New York in years. It had changed a lot in some respects, in others it looked exactly as I remembered, probably exactly as it had fifty or a hundred years before.

I walked to Sixth Avenue, then headed downtown. Sixth Avenue down to Fourteenth Street still looked the same, but it had changed, and for a moment I couldn't put my finger on it. Then it hit me, and I smiled to myself. I was getting so cosmopolitan I didn't notice some things any more. Sixth Avenue from Twenty-third Street to Fourteenth was almost entirely Puerto Rican. The conversations I heard around me were, for the most part, in Spanish.

The bars were in the same places, but now they bore Spanish names: El Grotto, El Cerrado, El Portoqueno. The old Italian delicatessens were still there as I had remembered, but now they were *bodegas,* with more fruit and fewer vegetables. If anything, Sixth Avenue was cleaner than it ever had been and the round-hipped, vivacious Latin girls clacking by on their high heels were a big improvement over the slow-moving eddies of elderly ladies with their shopping bags who used to fill the neighborhood.

Fourteenth Street looked more like Calle Catorce in San Juan, but there was an abrupt change from there southward to Third Street. Here, it was much as it had always been, the small-business part of the Village, hardware stores, drugstores, grocery stores, delicatessens, ten-cent stores, coffee shops. There never had been any particular ethnic identity to this stretch of the avenue and there wasn't now.

It was a polyglot crowd; neatly suited business men with attaché cases, strolling hippies with shoulder-length hair and blue jeans, chic housewives pushing black plastic baby carriages, hobbling old ladies with gnarled features and vacant eyes, kids armed with baseball gloves, a beggar on crutches. There were more mixed couples than I had remembered.

At Third Street, I turned east past MacDougal and Sullivan, then went south again on Thompson Street, a big grin of reminiscence on my face. Thompson Street never changes. All the way down to Prince Street, it is the old

Italian Village: quiet tree-lined streets bordered with solid rows of brownstones, each with its series of steps running up to heavy oaken front doors, each one fronted by an iron railing designed to keep the unwary from falling onto the steep row of concrete steps leading to the cellar. For some reason, when the Village was built up in the late 1880s the cellar doors were always put in the front instead of the back.

Here, the pace is different than anywhere else in the city. The noise seems suffused, the action slower. Old men stand in clusters of two and three, never sitting on the stoop, just standing, talking their dotage away; fat-breasted housewives lean from upper windows to chat with neighbors standing on the sidewalk below.

On the fenced-in playground of St. Theresa's Junior High School, the neighborhood's young Italian bucks, long out of school, mingle with the kids in a perpetual softball game. On the sidewalks, the black-eyed, black-haired Italian girls walk sturdily, eyes straight ahead, if they are alone. If they are with a group of girls, they squirm and dawdle, talking constantly, darting their eyes up and down the street, making it ring with their laughter.

There are few businesses on Thompson Street, an occasional candy store, inevitably dark green with a faded, half-slashed awning sheltering the newspaper stand; a delicatessen or two, with huge salamis hanging in the windows; here and there a drugstore, almost always on the corner. What Thompson does have, however, is funeral parlors—three of them. You go to one if you are a friend of the Ruggieros, another if you are a friend of the Franzinis, the third one if you have no connections with either family or, if you do, don't want them known.

Also on Thompson, between Houston Street and

Spring, there are five restaurants, good Italian restaurants, with neatly checkered tableclothes, a candle on each table, a small bar along one wall of the adjoining room. The people of the neighborhood often drink at the bars, but they never eat at the tables. They eat at home every night, every meal. Yet somehow the restaurants are full every evening, though they never advertise—they just seem to draw couples, each of whom has somehow discovered their own little Italian restaurant.

By the time I reached Spring Street and turned left toward West Broadway, I was so deep in the Old Italian ambiance I almost forgot that my involvement was something less than pleasant. The grand old Italian families who live south of Houston Street are not, unfortunately, mutually exclusive of the Mafia.

I arrived at *Franzini Olive Oil* at exactly two o'clock. Louie's cousin Philomina wore a white sweater that emphasized her breasts, and a brown suede skirt that buttoned down the front only partially so that when she moved, a good deal of well-shaped leg was showing. It was rather more than I'd expected from the conservatively-dressed Philomina of the day before, but I'm not one to complain about a very attractive girl wearing more revealing clothes.

She showed me into Popeye's office with a polite smile and an impersonal air she might have used for the window cleaner or the cleaning lady.

Louie was already there, bouncing. He'd been talking to Popeye. Now he turned, wrung my hand in a fervent handshake as if he hadn't seen me in months, and placed the other hand on my shoulder. "Hi ya, Nick! How are you? Good to see you!"

The huge old man in his wheelchair behind the black desk glared at me. Reluctantly he nodded and motioned with one hand. "Sit down." I took one straight chair, sat back, and crossed my legs. Louie took the other, spun it around, and then sat down straddling it, his arms crossed over the back.

Popeye Franzini shook his head slightly, as if Louie were a puzzle he could never figure out. Fat fingers fumbled at a cigar box on his desk and stripped the cellophane from a long black cheroot. He stuck the cigar in his mouth, lit it from the cigarette lighter on his desk and then peered at me through the smoke.

"Louie seems to think you're pretty damned good."

I shrugged. "I can handle myself. I've been around."

He stared at me a moment, evaluating a piece of merchandise. Then he apparently made up his mind. "Okay, okay," he muttered. He fumbled on both sides of his wheelchair as if looking for something, then raised his head and bellowed:

"Philomina! Philomina! Dammit! You got my briefcase?"

Louie's cousin appeared immediately, though her exquisite grace prevented her movements from seeming hurried. She placed a battered old grey attaché case in front of Popeye and glided out silently.

"You seen that goddamned Larry?" he grumbled at Louie as he flipped open the clasps. "He ain't been around all day."

Louie spread both hands, palms up. "I haven't seen him since yesterday, Uncle Joe."

"Me neither," the old man growled.

Thank God! That meant Spelman hadn't communicated with the Franzinis before coming up to roust me. I could probably thank the effects of heroin for that lapse of procedure.

Popeye Franzini took a sheaf of papers from the attaché case, studied the first page for a moment, and then laid them down on top of the case in front of him. His voice, his whole manner, suddenly changed and he was now the businessman.

"Frankly, Nick, you're not the man I would pick for this job. We don't know you well enough and I would prefer someone who had been with the organization. However, Louie here says he wants you, and if he thinks he can trust you, that's the main thing."

I returned his gaze without expression. "Whatever you say, Don Joseph."

He nodded. Of course whatever he said. "The point is," he went on, "this organization has been having some difficulties lately. Our receipts are off, a lot of our people are getting into trouble with the cops, the Ruggieros are moving in left and right. In other words, somehow or another we seem to have lost our grip on things. When that happens in a business organization you call in an efficiency expert and make some changes. Well, I consider us a business organization and I'm going to do just that."

Popeye Franzini drew hard on his cigar and then pointed it through the smoke at Louie. "There's my efficiency expert."

I looked at Louie, remembering how my impressions of him had changed so quickly in Beirut. Outwardly, his demeanor suggested anything but efficiency. I was beginning to grow fond of this man. Though I was sure he was more intelligent than he appeared at first, I doubted he was very tough.

As though reading my thoughts, Popeye went on. "Louie's a lot tougher than most people think. I brought him up that way. Like he was my own son." His face grimaced in a smile at his nephew, who grinned back at him. "Right, Louie?"

"Right, Uncle Joe." He spread his hands expressively, his dark face beaming.

The Franzini story played through my mind as I listened with one ear to Popeye's obviously oft-repeated story of Louie growing up as the man he'd raised him to be.

Up until the second World War, the three Franzini brothers had been a team. Louie's father, Luigi, was killed during the Marine landing at Guadalcanal in August, 1942; the young Louie was taken in by Joseph.

By that time Joseph was battling the ravages of MS, though he was still able to walk with a lurching gait and drive a car. He also had his older brother, Alfredo, to contend with; the two brothers had grown steadily apart, and after Luigi's death, their quarrels grew into a bitter war for control of the family interests.

If the schism between the brothers had continued the entire Franzini *famiglia* as a Mafia power center would have been undermined. Joseph wasn't about to let that happen. In February, 1953, he set up a peace parley with Alfredo. On the day of the meeting, he took his Cadillac, alone, to pick up Alfredo, and the two brothers drove east, out of the Village.

It was the last time anyone ever saw Alfredo Franzini.

Joseph maintained—still did—that after they visited Alfredo's New Jersey place, he drove his brother back to the city, leaving him off on Sullivan Street—the spot where he'd picked him up. No one had ever been able to prove otherwise. Officially, Alfredo Franzini had been kidnapped off the streets of New York by persons unknown. Unofficially, the authorities knew better.

Only Joseph Franzini could support their suspicions, and Joseph Franzini never wavered from his story.

Joseph had made a great show of vowing vengeance against whoever had abducted his brother. He took Alfredo's wife, Maria Rosa, into his own home—"for protection," he said—along with her daughter, Philomina, who was just three years old at the time. Maria Rosa had died two years later of cancer, but Joseph had continued to care for his two brothers' children as if they were his own. He had never married.

Popeye Franzini continued to talk, an articulate mountain of flesh encased in a chrome and canvas cage with spoked wheels.

". . . So then I sent Louie on to Columbia and he graduated *magna cum laude*. Since then, he's been running the Franzini Olive Oil business, and that's just about the only thing we have going that is producing the amount of revenue that it should."

"What did you study, Louie?" I was curious.

He grinned self-consciously. "Business administration. That's why Uncle Joe thinks I might be able to straighten out some of our operations."

"What operations are we talking about?" I asked the old man.

He glared at me.

"Look," I said. "If you want me to work with Louie, I have to know what we're getting into. You forget, I just got here yesterday."

He nodded. "All right. We're talking right now about porno, securities, numbers, trucks, vending machines, laundry supply, and narcotics."

"No prostitution?"

He waved the idea away disdainfully. "We leave that to the flashy black pimps." He looked thoughtful. "We do have other operations, of course, but those I named are the ones we're having trouble with."

I turned to Louie. "You done your homework on these?"

He sighed and looked a little embarrassed. "Well . . ."

Popeye explained. "Louie's never been in any of the operations. I worked hard at keeping him out, except for olive oil, and that's legit."

I tried to keep from smiling. In the Red Fez in Beirut, after I had pulled my trump with the tube of heroin, Louie's manner had implied that he was right in there, one of his Uncle's men behind all the Franzini rackets. In reality, he knew almost nothing about their inner workings. And Franzini wanted him to straighten out the "operations"? My skepticism must have shown.

"Yeah. I know," Popeye said. "It sounds crazy, maybe. But the way things have been going . . . something has to be done. I think Louie can do it by streamlining our business practices."

I shrugged. "It's your ball game. Where do I come in?"

"Louie here is my efficiency expert. I want you—somebody new to the organization—to provide the muscle. These guys all work for me, and they do what I say. But sometimes they have to be convinced more directly. They're not going to want Louie poking around in their operations because they're probably cheating me somewhere along the line—I know that. If Louie goes by himself, they're going to try to bamboozle him. If you go along, they'll know I sent you just to let them know this is coming straight from me and no shit about it."

For the job I was supposed to be doing for Uncle Sam, it was a heaven-sent opportunity. "Okay. Now, you mentioned porno, securities, numbers, trucks, vending machines, laundry supply and narcotics. What is 'trucks'?"

The old man grasped both wheels of his wheelchair with gross hands and moved himself back from the desk a foot or so before he answered. " 'Trucks' is what we call our hijacking operation run by Joe Polito. It's mostly garment district stuff, once in a while a little hardware like TV sets or stoves. We took three hundred stoves out of Brooklyn the other day. But it's been going bad. The cops, the feds, even the Ruggieros, everybody's cracking down."

"The Ruggieros?" I was amused. If he thought he was having trouble with the Ruggieros now, wait until he got that package with Larry Spelman's clothes in it!

He dismissed the Ruggieros with a wave of his hand. "Nothing big. Some of our boys picked up a garment truck the other day, then a couple of Ruggiero's boys hijacked *our* boys."

"I thought things were coordinated between the families in New York."

He nodded a massive head. "Usually. This time, Ruggiero said it was a mistake, that his boys pulled the job independently."

I laughed. "You believe that?"

He glared back at me. Levity was not part of Popeye Franzini's way of life. "Yeah, I do. Once in a while you have to let the boys go off on their own. You try to control them a hundred percent, and you're asking for a lot of internal troubles."

I could see his point. "What about the other operations?"

"Pretty much the same thing. Nothing I can put my finger on; things just seem to be going badly. I think it may be because over the years we've gotten too loose, spent too much time trying to do things legit. We did better when we played it tough. That's what I want to get back to. Play it tough! Good business procedures, but tough!"

He paused. "By the way, you can use Locallo and Manitti if you need them. Just give them a week or two to get used to the city, that's all."

"Right."

"That reminds me." He half-spun in his wheelchair, so that he was pointed toward the doorway. "Philomina!" he shouted. "Philomina! Did we get that Beirut report yet?"

She appeared immediately in the doorway. "No," she said quietly. "Nothing yet." She disappeared again.

"Goddamn!" he exploded. "That report was due in yesterday and isn't here yet! I can't find Larry any god-damned place! The whole goddamned business is falling apart!"

He didn't know the half of it yet, I thought to myself.

It was remarkable the way he could switch from one personality to the other, from the cool, self-appraising businessman with the carefully structured sentences to the shouting, fuming Italian tyrant, petulant when things didn't go his way, morose when they did.

Now he pounded a fist on the armrest of his wheel-chair. "Goddamn! You got to get this straightened out. Now! And find Larry, too. He's probably on a goddamned heroin nod somewhere. I got to have him. Get the hell out of here and go find him!"

Louie got up and started for the door, but stopped when he saw I'd remained seated.

The old man glared. "Well?"

I shrugged. "I'm sorry, Don Joseph. But I can't work for nothing. I need some money up front."

He snorted. "Money! Hell! You stay with me, you'll get plenty of money." He regarded me somberly for a moment, then turned toward the doorway again. "Philomina!" he yelled. "Give this new guy some money. Give him a big one." He spun his wheelchair again in my direction. "Now get out of here, dammit! I got things to do."

"Thanks." I got up.

"And I want to see you at the party tonight."

"Yes, sir."

He was still glaring as we left the office, a huge old man in a wheelchair, a weird combination of helplessness and power.

I went to where his niece was counting out some bills on her desk and stared at her face—and the white sweater. She paid no attention.

"Here." She handed me a sheaf of bills. I could have been the paperboy getting fifteen cents for *The New York Times*.

I leafed through the bills. Twenty fifties.

"Thank you, Philomina," I said politely. "Your uncle pays very well, doesn't he?"

"My uncle sometimes overpays," she said snippily, emphasizing the "over."

She looked past me to Louie with a sudden smile. "I'll see you tonight, Louie. I'm awfully glad you're back."

"Sure, Phil," Louie replied, looking embarrassed.

Outside on the sidewalk, we walked along together. "What's with your cousin, Louie? Should I change my after-shave or what?"

He laughed. "Oh, don't pay any attention to Philomina. She does a great job for the olive oil business, but whenever she gets into . . . uh . . . other operations, she gets up on her high horse. She doesn't want anything to do with it, really."

"What the hell does that mean? She's old enough to know she can't have it both ways, isn't she?"

He laughed nervously, hands jammed deep in his pockets as we strode along. "Well, it's not really both ways as far as Philomina is concerned. It's just that once in a while she has to give somebody some money or something, like she just did you. Usually, we don't conduct organization business in that office. I guess we did today just because Larry disappeared somewhere and wasn't around to take Uncle Joe over to the Counting House."

"The Counting House?"

"It's over on Spring. It's a big old building we use to keep our records in. Kind of a headquarters."

We walked along in silence for a few minutes. Then Louie spoke up again. "Where do you suppose we can find Larry?"

"Don't ask me. Hell, I just got here yesterday."

"Yeah. I forgot." He clapped me on the shoulder. "Look, why don't you go back to the hotel and get some rest. We'll see you over at the restaurant tonight . . . about nine o'clock."

It sounded like a fine idea to me. I certainly had no desire to go off looking for Spelman. Particularly since I knew where he was. "Great," I replied with unfeigned enthusiasm.

He went off cheerfully, whistling, his hands in his pockets, heading for the subway, I guessed. I hailed a cab and went back to the Chelsea.

Once back at the hotel, I called Jack Gourlay at the *News*. It seemed strange giving my right name over the phone to the operator.

"Nick Carter!" Jack's slow voice repeated. "When the hell did you get back to town?"

"A while ago," I hedged. "Listen, Jack, I want a favor."

"Sure. What can I do for you?"

"I wonder if you could slip into a story somewhere that Larry Spelman is missing and that the Franzinis think the Ruggieros might have something to do with it."

The best way to get someone to think something sometimes, is to tell them what they are supposed to be thinking.

On the other end of the line, Jack whistled. "Get it into a story, hell! I'll make it a story! But is it true, Nick? Is he really missing?"

"He's really missing," I said.

"And do the Franzinis think . . . ?"

"I don't know," I answered quite honestly. "But I'd like them to."

He was quiet for a moment, then, "You know, something like that could start another gang war in town. Those two families haven't been getting along so well lately."

"I know."

"Okay, Nick. As long as you're sure Spelman is really missing."

"He's missing. Really."

"Okay, man, you're on. Anything else I should know?"

"No, Jack. But I really appreciate it. I'm kind of busy now; maybe we can get together for dinner or drinks one of these nights when I get clear."

"Love to," he said, and hung up. Get Jack Gourlay started on a story and he doesn't want to fool around with small talk.

I stretched out on my bed and took a nap.

CHAPTER 10

I arrived at Tony's Garden for Philomina's party at about nine o'clock that night and my first impression was that I should have called the FBI instead of Jack Gourlay. The place was so packed with Italian hoods it looked like a 1937 rally for Benito Mussolini.

Usually, Tony's is a quiet little bar-restaurant that once was a hangout for has-been and would-be writers and is now a mecca for the current crop of Village bohemians and hippies high on philosophy, low on cash. The iron-barred peephole in the back door attested to the fact that it had been a speakeasy back in Prohibition days.

It is always dark, with black walls trimmed in dark brown and all the light subdued. The dining room is fair-sized, but overcroweded with rough-hewn tables. Once past the tables, a small barroom is squared off with elbow-level counters and a row of undecorative coathooks. All in all, it is dark, dingy, and devoid of decor, but for years it has been one of the most popular places in the Village.

My first surprise was the number of people jammed

into the place. The tables had all been removed except for three long ones in front of the fireplace which were piled high with Italian pasta of unbelievable variety. It was a standup party with buffet dining and an open bar, everyone with glass or dish in hand. From the barroom a small combo enthusiastically played Italian songs.

Don Joseph Franzini and his guests of honor were the only ones seated, lined up in a row behind piles of long-stemmed roses that covered the top of a single long table set up in the corner. It was Philomina's birthday party, but Franzini held the place of honor, a great mass of flesh enclosed in tuxedo elegance. Philomina Franzini sat on his right and next to her a large, buxom woman I didn't recognize. Louie sat on Franzini's left and next to him a short, portly man with a cherubic face and soft, snow-white hair.

A small crowd pressed around the table, shaking hands, paying their respects, introducing the old man to this one or that one. The attention all centered on Franzini; his niece sat lovely and demure, a set smile on her face, rarely saying a word. But as I edged closer, I saw there were dozens of small white envelopes interspersed among the roses. As I watched, a couple more were tossed onto the table.

I was puzzling over that phenomenon when Louie spotted me on the edge of the crowd. He immediately jumped to his feet and came over.

"Hiya, Nick! How are you? Good to see ya!"

"Hi, Louie." He took my elbow and ushered me into the barroom. "Let's have a drink. I get claustrophobic sitting there with all those people closing in around me."

I ordered a brandy and soda. Louie drank the same thing he'd had in Beirut, red wine.

We leaned against the back wall to keep from being

trampled on. "Some party, huh?" he grinned. "I'll bet we've got a hundred fifty people here, and at least a hundred of them are already drunk."

He was right about that. I neatly sidestepped a tall, tuxedo-clad figure as he staggered past us, glass in hand, one lock of hair down over his forehead. "Mariateresa," he was calling rather plaintively. "Has anyone seen Mariateresa?"

Louie laughed and shook his head. "In a couple of hours, it really ought to be great."

"It sure looks different than I remember it." I looked around the once-familiar room now reverberating with sound. When I had known it years before, it had been a place for a quiet beer and an even quieter chess game.

"I didn't know this was one of your places," I said.

Louie laughed, naturally. "It isn't. We own some seventeen restaurants on the lower west side and another dozen or so, say, are 'affiliates,' but Tony's isn't one of them."

"Then why hold Philomina's party here instead of one of your own?"

He clapped me on the shoulder and laughed again. "It's easy, Nick. See all these guys here? Now, some of them are all right, good solid businessmen, friends of the family, that sort of thing."

I nodded and he went on. "On the other hand, there are also a lot of guys here you might call—uh—hoods. Understand?"

I nodded again. I couldn't deny him that. Dozens of rough looking types were talking, drinking, singing, shouting, or just standing morosely in corners. They looked like they had been recruited from Central Casting for a latter-day Al Capone movie. And from the bulging jackets I had observed, there were more guns in the place than the Russians had been able to muster against the British at Balaklava.

"What's that got to do with holding a party here instead of one of your own places?"

"Simple. We don't want to give one of our own places a bad name. If the cops wanted to, you know, they could raid this place tonight and pick up a lot of what they call 'undesirable characters.' They wouldn't be guilty of anything, of course, and they'd eventually have to let them go. It would just be harassment, but it would make nice headlines in the papers. It would be bad for business."

A tipsy little redhead with freckles across the bridge of her nose had been working her way across the crowded room with two black-browed bullies in tow. She came to a stop in front of Louie, threw one arm around his neck, and gave him a big kiss.

"Hi, Louie, you cute li'l ol' thing. Who's your handsome friend here?" She was cute, even if she was one of those fashionable girls who have the body of a fourteen-year-old boy—and she had an exciting awareness of her own sexuality. She was looking at me hungrily. Her two companions glowered, but I returned her look. Her eyes were saying she didn't care what the rest of the world thought and mine were saying, okay, if that's what you want.

Louie made the introductions. Her name was Rusty Pollard and she was a lay teacher at St. Teresa's. One of the gorillas with her was named Jack Baity, the other, Rocco something-or-other. Baity made some crude remarks about *lay* teachers, but Rusty and I were having too good a time discovering each other.

She was an outrageous flirt.

"What's a big hunk of guy like you doing here with all

these little squat Italians?" she asked, one hand cocked on a slim, outthrust hip, her head thrown back.

I looked at her in mock dismay. "Little squat Italians? Keep that up and you'll end up in tomorrow's pizza pie."

She dismissed the possibility with an airy wave of her hand. "Ah, they're harmless."

I looked Rusty over carefully. "What's a nice girl like you doing here with all these little squat Italians?"

Rusty laughed. "You'd better not let Mr. Franzini hear you refer to Philomina as a little squat Italian or *you'll* end up on someone's pizza pie."

I shrugged, offered her a cigarette and lit it for her. "You didn't answer my question."

She gestured at the table where Franzini sat with his niece. "Maybe one of these days I can collect some of those little white envelopes myself."

I saw that now they were stacked neatly in front of Philomina instead of being scattered around the sheaves of roses. "What the hell are they?" I asked. "Cards?"

"Your name is Nick Canzoneri and you don't know what those are?" she asked.

"Of course," I hedged, "but you tell me Miss non-little-squat-Italian Pollard. I just want to see if you know."

She laughed. "The games people play. Every one of those little envelopes contains a check from one of Mr. Franzini's associates. Even the little guys have dug up what they could. It's all for Philomina's birthday. She's probably got seven or eight thousand dollars there."

"And you'd like the same thing?"

"Maybe one of these days one of these squat little Italians is going to offer me something besides a weekend in Atlantic City, and when he does I'm going to grab him. And when I do, I'm eventually going to end up sitting at a table full of roses going through a lot of little white envelopes."

"About that weekend in Atlantic . . ." I started to say, but across the room, Popeye Franzini was glowering at me and waving an imperious arm in a gesture that brooked no hesitation.

I half bowed toward Rusty. "Sorry, honey. Caesar beckons. Maybe I'll catch up with you later."

Her lips puckered in a pout. "Rat!" But her eyes were still challenging.

I pushed across the crowded floor and paid my respects to Franzini and Philomina.

The flush of wine was on his face and his speech was thick. "Hav'n' a good time?"

"Yes, sir."

"Good, good." He put one arm around Philomina's shoulders. "I wan' you to take my li'l girl home." He squeezed her shoulders and she seemed to shrink just a bit, her eyes downcast, not looking at either one of us. "She don't feel s'good, but th' party's jus' startin'. So you take her home, huh?"

He turned to Philomina. "Right, honey?"

She looked up at me. "I'd appreciate it, Mr. Canzoneri."

I bowed. "Of course."

"Thank you." She rose demurely. "Thank you, Uncle Joe. It's been just wonderful, but I do feel dizzy." She leaned over and kissed the old toad on the cheek. I felt like gagging.

"Right! Right!" he roared. He pinned me with bleary eyes. "Take good care my li'l girl."

I nodded. "Yes, sir." Philomina and I maneuvered through the crowd toward the door. She murmured a few good nights here and there, but no one seemed to pay her much attention, even though it was ostensibly her party.

We finally squeezed through and got out the door on Bedford Street. The fresh air tasted good. Philomina and I each took a deep breath, then smiled at each other. She was wearing an off-the-shoulder evening dress of pure white except for a bright slash of flame red running diagonally across the front. Her gloves and stole matched the red slash. Striking.

I remained respectful. "Would you like to stop for coffee, first, Miss Franzini, or would you rather go directly home?"

"Home, please." Miss Franzini was being icy again. I shrugged and we set off. At Seventh Avenue and Barrow Street I was able to hail a cab.

It was only ten minutes to Philomina's apartment house—London Terrace—and we rode in regal silence to the awning marking the entrance.

I paid the cab and got out, then helped Philomina out. She pulled her arm away. "This will do," she said coldly. "Thank you very much."

I grabbed her elbow a little roughly, pivoted her and directed her toward the door. "I'm sorry, Miss Franzini. When Popeye Franzini tells me to take you home, I take you all the way home."

She could understand that, I guess, but felt she didn't have to reply. We went up the elevator in cold silence, while the elevator man tried to pretend to himself that we weren't there.

We got off on the seventeenth floor and I followed her down to her door, 17-E.

She took her key from her purse and looked at me coldly. "Good night, Mr. Canzoneri."

I smiled gently, and firmly took the key out of her hand. "Sorry, Miss Franzini. Not yet. I want to use your telephone."

"You can use the one in the bar down the street."

I smiled again as I put the key in the lock and opened the door. "I'd rather use yours." There wasn't much she could do about it. I was just about twice her size.

Philomina flicked on a light in the small foyer, then led the way into a neatly furnished living room and turned on one of the two floor lamps flanking a comfortable looking sofa. I perched on one end of the couch, picked up the phone and dialed a number.

Philomina gave me a dirty look, crossed her arms and leaned against the opposite wall. She wasn't even going to take that stole off until I got out of there.

It was after midnight, but I let the phone ring. The telephone at AXE's central information section is manned twenty-four hours a day. Finally, a girl's voice answered. "Six-nine-oh-oh."

"Thank you," I said. "Would you charge this call to my credit card number, please? H-281-766-5502." The last four numbers were the key of course, my serial number as AXE's No. 1 agent.

"Yes sir," said the voice on the other end.

"I need a red file check," I said. Philomina could hear everything I was saying, of course, but she couldn't possibly make much sense out of it. A red file check was a checkout on the highly secret list of confidential FBI agents. The white file was for CIA, blue for the National Security Agency, but I was playing a hunch it was red I wanted.

"Yes, sir," the girl on the telephone said.

"New York," I said. "Philomina Franzini. F-r-a-n-z-i-n-i." I looked over at her and gave a slight smile. She was standing with arms akimbo, balled fists pressed against her hips, her eyes snapping.

"Just a moment, sir."

It was more than a moment, but I waited patiently, Philomina watching.

The voice came back on. "Philomina Franzini, sir? F-r-a-n-z-i-n-i?"

"Yes."

"That is affirmative, sir. Red File. Status C-Seven. Four years. Class Twelve. The Franzini Olive Oil Company. Do you understand Status and Class, sir?"

She would have explained them, but I knew, all right. Philomina had been an FBI agent for four years. Status C-7 meant she was one of those thousands of FBI informers who are volunteers, and never are in contact with any other agents except the single man in charge of them. Class 12 meant she was never to be asked for action, nor was she to have access to any classified information about the Bureau.

Jack Gourlay once told me there were thousands of Status C-7 agents—informers would be a better word—working for legitimate companies around New York City, filing regular monthly reports on the business operation. Ninety-five percent, he said, never turned up anything of value, but the other five percent made all the drudgery of sifting through reports worthwhile.

I put the phone down and turned to Philomina.

"Well, what do you know," I said. "Aren't you the nice little girl, though?"

"What do you mean?"

"Spying on your own uncle. Now, that just isn't right, Philomina."

She turned white. One hand flew to her mouth and she nibbled at the back of a knuckle. "What do you mean?"

"Just what I said. Spying on your uncle for the FBI."

"That's crazy! I don't know what you're talking about!"

She looked terrified, and I couldn't blame her. As far as

she knew, I was just another hood about to hook up with the Franzini family. What I was saying could destroy her. There was no point in tormenting her. I started to tell her, then stopped.

She had made one slight movement, as if holding back a sob, her hands fumbling beneath the flame red stole. Then suddenly there was a small, ugly gun in her hand, a Saturday Night Special. It was pointed directly at me. The muzzle looked enormous.

I threw up my hands in a hurry. "Hey, wait a minute! Wait a minute!"

The look of frightened panic that had made me feel sorry for her a moment before was now gone. There was a cold, almost vicious look to her black eyes and that soft, sensuous mouth was drawn into a taut line.

She gestured with the ugly little gun. "Sit down!"

"Now, wait . . ."

"I said, *sit down.*"

I turned to sit on the sofa, bending slightly as most people when they start to sit on something as deeply settling as a couch. Then, with one swinging movement I grabbed the tight blue pillow decorating the back of the couch and slung it at her as I dove headlong over the end of the couch.

The Saturday Night Special roared in my ear and a bullet slammed into the wall just above my head.

On the floor now, I rolled into a fast crouch and sprung at where she must be standing, my head thrust forward like a battering ram, slamming into her stomach.

But she sidestepped neatly. I had a momentary glimpse of the gun, flashing up, and then down. Something crashed against the back of my ear and my head exploded in a great flash of red pain and black nothingness.

When I came to, I was flat on my back on the living

room floor. Philomina Franzini sat astride my body. I was groggily aware that her skirt was pulled up high over her hips, but only groggily. I was much more acutely aware of the fact that the muzzle of the gun was jammed into my mouth. The cold metal was hard and tasteless against my teeth.

I blinked my eyes to clear the film from them.

Despite her unladylike position, Philomina's voice was coldly efficient.

"All right. Talk. I want to know who you called and why. Then I'm turning you over to the FBI. Understand? And if I have to, I'll kill you."

I looked up at her bleakly.

"Talk!" she gritted. She moved the gun back just enough so it wasn't gagging me, but the muzzle of it still brushed against my lips. Philomina seemed to prefer point-blank range.

"Talk!" she demanded.

I didn't have much choice. As Class 12, she wasn't supposed to get any classified information. And I was certainly classified. On the other hand, she had that damned pistol jammed in my face and to go through the charade of having her turn me into the FBI seemed sort of silly.

I began talking.

It's hard to be earnest when you're flat on your back with a well-packed and vibrant girl sitting on your chest and a gun barrel nudging your lips. But I tried. I tried very hard.

"Okay, honey. You win, but take it easy."

She glared at me.

I tried again. "Look, we're on the same side of this thing. Honest! Who do you think I just called? I was just calling the FBI to check on you."

"What made you do that?"

"Something you said. The way you hate everything here and still stick around. There had to be a reason."

She shook her head, lips pursed. "Why would you call the FBI, instead of Uncle Joe?"

"Like I said, we're on the same side of this thing."

The Saturday Night Special didn't waver, but her thinking must have. "What's the FBI number?" she snapped.

That was easy. "Two-two-two, six-six-five-four."

"What did they tell you?"

I told her, Class and Status, all that stuff. And I kept talking, fast. I couldn't give her classified details, but I told her about Ron Brandenburg and Madeleine Leston in the FBI office, to show her my familiarity with it. I didn't tell her I was with AXE, or what my mission was, but I told her enough that she began to get the idea. Gradually, the muzzle of the gun began to retreat from my face.

As I finished, she gave a wrenching sob and laid the gun on the floor alongside my head. Covering her eyes with both hands, she began to cry.

"Easy, honey. Easy." I reached up to grasp her shoulders and pulled her down over me, so that I could hook my hand behind her head. She was unresisting and I rolled her over, off my chest, so that we were side by side on the floor, her head resting on my arm, my other arm around her.

"Easy, Philomina, take it easy." She was still crying, unrestrainedly now. I could feel her round breasts against my chest. Cupping my fingers under her chin, I raised her face away from my shoulder. Tears streamed down her cheeks.

There is only one way for a man to stop a woman from crying. I kissed her gently, reassuringly, holding her to me, kissing her again.

Gradually, the crying subsided and her body became

more compliant, relaxed. The unfeeling lips softened, then gradually, bit by bit, opened slightly, then more. Her tongue stroked mine, then her arms tightened around my neck.

I held her close, feeling the roundness of her breasts pressing against me. Gently, I kissed the wet eyelashes as I pulled away just enough to talk.

"Easy, honey, easy. Just take it easy," I murmured.

A shudder ran through her body, and she pulled my mouth back to hers, and now her tongue was a darting, live organ, probing deeply, her lips flattened against mine.

My right hand, pressing her to me, discovered the zipper on the back of her off-the-shoulder dress, and I gently tugged away at it, feeling the dress come apart under my fingers until they reached the small of her back, touched the delicate elastic of her panties.

I slid my hand under the panties and gently across her buttocks, so that the back of my hand pulled downward on them. Her hips lifted ever so slightly so that they were clear of the floor, and in a moment I had the panties off and discarded. With a single twist of the fingers, I unhooked her bra, and as I moved away so that I would have room to take it off, I could feel Philomina's fingers fumbling at my trousers.

In a moment, Philomina and I were both naked, and her face was buried in my shoulder. I carried her into the bedroom. For a luxurious minute, I contented myself with the feel of her bare breasts against my chest, then pulled her tightly to me, throbbing with desire.

Then Philomina began to move, slowly, gently at first, touching me, stroking me, her mouth wet and hot on mine. My muscles tensed, crying out for her, shuddering with anticipation.

She was moving faster now, intensity replacing subtlety,

flame burning the smoke away. With one great convulsive movement, I went over on top of her, pressing her down on the bed, driving in, ramming through, smashing down on her, consuming and being consumed.

She squirmed upward, writhing in ecstasy, her hands clutching my buttocks and pressing me into her. "Oh, my God!" she cried. "Oh, Jesus!" Her legs wrapped tightly around my waist as she heaved upward against my weight and I half-rose to my knees to accommodate her, sliding deeper, more exquisitely, then pumping wildly, frantically, and finally exploding in a great torrent of exultation.

CHAPTER 11

Later, still lying on the floor, she clung to me tightly. "Don't leave me, Nick. Please don't leave me. I'm so alone, and so scared."

She had been lonely and scared for a long time. She told me about it as we sat at the window table, watching a streaky dawn break in the east, and sipping at mugs of black coffee.

For years, growing up in the Franzini household on Sullivan Street as a little girl, she had had no concept that Popeye Franzini was anything except her kind and loving "Uncle Joe." From the time she was nine years old, he would take great delight in letting her push him in his wheelchair down to Washington Square Park on Sundays, where he used to like to feed the squirrels.

I sipped at my mug of coffee, and was reminded of one of life's more curious puzzles. Why is it that every woman who is extraordinary in bed is unable to brew a decent cup of coffee? A friend of mine used to say you could tell an overly sexy woman by the prominence of the veins on the back of her hand. But my experience has been that you can tell them by the lousy quality of their coffee.

Philomina's coffee tasted like chicory. I stood up and stepped over to her side of the table. I leaned over and kissed her softly on the lips. My hand slipped inside the blue robe she was now wearing and gently fondled her bare breast.

She leaned back in the chair for a moment, her eyes closed, long lashes soft against her cheek. "Mmmmmmm!" Then she pushed me away gently. "Go sit down and finish your coffee."

I shrugged. "If you'd rather."

She giggled. "Not really, but let's finish our coffee, anyway."

I gave her a mock look of male chauvinism rejected and sat down again. The coffee still tasted like chicory.

"When did you find out?" I asked.

"You mean about Uncle Joe?"

I nodded.

She cocked her head, thinking. "I guess I was about thirteen or so. There was a big story about Uncle Joe in *The New York Times Magazine*. We didn't read the *Times*. Nobody on Sullivan Street did. We all read the *Daily News*, but someone tore it out and sent it to me in the mail." She smiled. "At first, I just couldn't believe it. It said Uncle Joe was a Mafia boss, a gangster.

"I was terribly upset for a long time, even though I didn't really understand it all." She paused, her mouth tighter. "I know who sent it to me, too. At least I think I do."

I snorted. People don't usually carry teenage grudges into adulthood. "Who?" I asked.

She made a face. "Rusty Pollard."

"That thin red-headed girl in the green dress at the party?"

"That's the one." She sighed and let the tone of her voice ease off a bit. "Rusty and I went all the way through school together. We always hated each other. Still do, I guess. Though we're a little more grown up about it now."

"How come you always hated each other?"

Philomina shrugged. "Rich Italian, poor Irish, living next door to each other. What do you expect?"

"What happened after you read the story?" I asked.

"At first I didn't believe it, but in a way I had to. I mean, after all, it *was* in the *Times*. And I hated it! I just hated it! I used to love my Uncle Joe, and I used to feel so sorry for him in his wheelchair and everything, and then all of a sudden I couldn't stand him to touch me, or to be with me."

I was puzzled. "But you continued living with him."

She made a face. "I stayed with him because I had to. What's a thirteen-year-old girl going to do? Run away? And whenever I was the least bit disobedient, he'd beat me." Unconsciously, she rubbed her cheek, a long-forgotten bruise scarring her memory. "You learn in a hurry that way."

"Is that what made you go to the FBI?"

She poured herself another cup of the bitter coffee. "Of course not," she said after she had thought about it a moment.

"I hated the whole awful thing about killing and stealing and cheating, but I learned to live with it. I had to. I just decided that when I was eighteen, I would run away, join the Peace Corps, do something."

"Do most of the women in the—uh—family feel that way?"

"No. Most of them never think about it. They don't allow themselves to think about it. They were taught not to when they were little girls. It's the old Sicilian way: What the men do is no business of the women."

"But you were different?"

She nodded grimly. "I became fascinated by it. I found it repulsive, but I couldn't stay away from it. I read everything I could find in the library about the Mafia, the organization, the whole thing.

"That's why I stayed, and why I went to the FBI. Family ties. My father. Uncle Joe killed my father! Did you know that? He actually killed his own brother! My father."

"Do you know that for sure?"

She shook her head. "Not really, but once I read about the things that happened when I was three—I guess I was in high school at that time—I just knew it was true. It's something Uncle Joe would do, I just know it. And looking back, I'm sure my mother thought so, too. She only moved in with Uncle Joe because he forced her."

I stood up again and moved so that I could pull her head against my stomach. "You're quite a girl," I said softly. "Let's go back to bed."

She looked up and smiled, her eyes glistening. "Okay," she whispered. Then she managed a giggle. "I have to be in the office in a few hours."

"I won't waste any time," I promised.

Not taking her eyes from me, she stood up and loosened her belt so that the blue bathrobe fell open. I pressed her to me, my hands inside the open robe and against her body, stroking it slowly, exploring it. I lifted one breast and kissed the tightened nipple, then the other.

She groaned and rammed both hands down the front of my pants, grasping at me frantically but gently. I jerked in ecstasy, and in moments we were on the floor, writhing with passion.

Her lovemaking was as good as her coffee was bad.

After Philomina went to work that morning, I lazed around for a few hours, showered, dressed, then walked the two blocks down Twenty-third Street to the Chelsea. There was a note in my mail slot: *Call Mr. Franzini.*

There was also a wary look in the room clerk's eye. There aren't that many Franzinis around New York these days.

I thanked the clerk and went up to my room, looked the number up in the book and dialed.

Philomina answered. "Franzini Olive Oil."

"Hi."

"Oh, Nick," she breathed into the phone.

"What's up, honey?"

"Oh . . . oh, Mr. Canzoneri." Her voice was suddenly briskly efficient. Someone must have come into the office. "Yes," she went on. "Mr. Franzini would like to see you at two o'clock this afternoon."

"Well," I said, "at least it will give me a chance to see you."

"Yes, sir," she said briskly.

"You know I'm crazy about you."

"Yes, sir."

"Will you have dinner with me tonight?"

"Yes, sir."

". . . and then I'll take you home to bed."

"Yes, sir."

". . . and make love to you."

"Yes, sir. Thank you, sir." She hung up.

I grinned all the way down on the elevator. I smiled at the room clerk, which seemed to make him nervous. He had "made" me as an Organization hood and he wasn't a bit comfortable with the idea.

I went around the corner to the Angry Squire for brunch after picking up a copy of the *News* at the newsstand on the corner of Seventh Avenue.

Jack Gourlay's story was on page five.

HINT NEW GANG WAR IN MAFIA MYSTERY

The mysterious disappearance of Larry Spelman, reputed lieutenant to Mafia chief Joseph "Popeye" Franzini, may be the opening round of a new gang war here, according to Police Captain Hobby Miller.

Miller, in charge of the Department's Special Section for Organized Crime, said in an interview today that Spelman, Franzini's constant companion and bodyguard, had been missing from his usual haunts since the beginning of the week.

Captain Miller, according to the story, said rumors were rife in the underworld that Spelman had either been murdered, and his body disposed of, or had been kidnapped and was being held for ransom by the family headed by Gaetano Ruggiero.

Jack Gourlay had done a beautiful job.

I finished my brunch leisurely, basking in warm memories of Philomina and the thought that things were really going pretty well, as improbable as it had seemed when I first started.

I arrived at the Franzini Olive Oil Company offices promptly at two o'clock. Manitti and Locallo were there ahead of me, uncomfortable on the modern chairs. I smiled at Philomina when she ushered us into Popeye's office. She blushed, but avoided my eyes.

Today, Popeye looked a little older and a little fatter. The party the night before showed. Or perhaps it was the effect of Gourlay's story. A copy of the *News* lay on Franzini's desk. Leaning against the wall on the far side of the room, Louie looked nervous as the three of us arranged ourselves in front of his uncle's desk.

Popeye glowered at us, the hatred in his soul seething in his eyes.

He's upset about Spelman, I thought gleefully, but I was wrong.

"You, Locallo!" he barked.

"Yes, sir." The hood looked scared.

"Which one of you guys was the last one to see that Chinese broad, Su Lao Lin, in Beirut?"

Locallo spread his hands helplessly. "I dunno. Me and Manitti, we left together."

"I think it was Canzoneri here," Louie piped up, gesturing in my direction. "I left him there when I took Harold to the hospital." He glanced at me with a I-have-to-tell-the-truth look.

"Were you the last one there?" Popeye snapped.

I shrugged. "I don't know. I talked to her for a few minutes after Louie left, then she sent me over to see that guy Harkins, the penman."

"Do you know if she was expecting anyone after you left?"

I shook my head.

His eyes narrowed in thought, looking at me.

"Hmmmm! You musta been the last one to see Harkins, too."

He was getting too close for comfort, although I didn't really sense that I was in a lot of trouble at the moment. "No," I said innocently, "there was that other guy there. Came in right before I left. But, wait!" I feigned a look of sudden recollection. "I think he was the same guy I saw hanging around in the lobby of Miss Lin's hotel when I left." I pressed my fingers to my forehead. "Yeah, the same guy."

Popeye sat up straight, pounding a fist onto the desktop. "What guy?"

"Hell, I don't know if I remember. Let's see . . . Harkins introduced me. Fuggi, I think, or something like that . . . Fuggiero . . . I don't remember exactly."

"Ruggiero?" He fairly shot the words at me.

I snapped my fingers. "Yeah. That's it. Ruggiero."

"Goddamn! What was his first name?"

I shrugged. "Gee, I don't know. Bill, maybe, or Joe, or something like that."

"And you say you saw him in the hotel?"

I spread my hands, palms up. "Yeah. He was in the lobby, waiting for the elevator, when I came out. I remember now, I recognized him later when he came into Harkins' place."

"What did he look like?"

"You know, kind of average. He was dark . . ." I pretended to concentrate, frowning thoughtfully. I might as well make it good while I was at it. "I guess about five-foot-ten, kind of dark skin. Oh yeah, I remember. He was wearing a dark blue suit."

Popeye shook his head. "He don't sound familiar, but there's so many goddamned Ruggieros, it's hard to tell." He slammed his fist on the desktop again, then spun his wheelchair so he was looking directly at Louie. "That Chinese broad say anything about the Ruggieros to you?"

Louie shook his head. "No, sir, not a word." He hesitated. "What happened, Uncle Joe?"

Popeye glared at him in a fury. "They got blown up! That's what happened! Some son of a bitch went in there just after you guys took off and blew the goddamned place up. A bomb, for Chrissake! Vinnie just called from Beirut. He says it's all over the papers there."

"What about Su Lao Lin?"

"Dead as a goddamned doornail, Vinnie says."

Louie was as upset as his uncle now, arms akimbo on his hips, head thrust forward. I wondered if he'd made love to her, too.

"Anyone else hurt?"

Popeye shook his head, almost as if he were disappointed. "Nah. Except that goddamned Charlie Harkins got shot."

"Is he dead, too?"

Popeye nodded. "Yeah."

Louie frowned. "You think the Ruggieros did it?" Good boy, Louie, I applauded silently.

"Of course I think the Ruggieros did it," Popeye roared. "What the hell you think? Canzoneri here sees a Ruggiero in the dame's hotel, then meets him at Harkins' joint. Then there are two dead bodies. You don't think there's a connection? You think maybe it's just a coincidence?"

"No, no, Uncle Joe," Louie placated. "Except I don't know why the Ruggieros would knock them off. We even brought in a few guys for them through Beirut. It doesn't make any sense unless they're just out to get us."

"Goddamn! What the hell do you think?" Popeye

icked up the newspaper from his desk and waved it. "Did you read the goddamned paper this morning?"

Louie shrugged. "I don't know, Uncle Joe. Larry's een missing before when he's gone off on a jag. That tory could just be a lot of bull. You know how Hobby Miller is. That guy Gourlay can make him say anything e wants."

But the old man was not to be put down. He waved the aper again. "What about Beirut, then, smart-alec? What bout it?"

Louie nodded, trying to puzzle it out. "Yeah, I know. The two together are just too much. I guess they're going ut to get us all right, but Jeez! just a few weeks ago everything seemed to be going all right."

"Goddamn!" The old man pounded one fist into the alm of his other hand. "It don't sound all right to me!"

Louie shook his head. "I know, I know, Uncle Joe. But a street war doesn't make sense right now. We got enough roubles."

"We gotta do something! I ain't going to take that kind of shit from nobody," Popeye shouted.

"Okay, okay," Louie said. "So what do you want us to do?"

The old man's eyes narrowed, and he backed a half-urn away from his desk. "Kill me someone, goddamn! ust a little one, maybe. I don't want no Ruggiero. Not et I don't. I just want 'em to know we don't mess around." The hate in Popeye's eyes leaped with excitement now. The old man could smell blood. His fat hand clenched the rollbar of his wheelchair. "Go on, goddammit," he shouted. "Get moving!"

CHAPTER 12

Louie and I sat hunched over cups of *cappuchino* in the Decima Coffee House on West Broadway.

The walls were a chocolate brown, and the worn linoleum on the floor, perhaps green years ago, was a filthy black. A dozen oversized, gilt-framed paintings hung from the walls, their canvases barely distinguishable through a patina of fly specks and grease. A dirty glass counter showcase displayed a tired collection of pastries—*napole one, baba al rum, mille foglie, cannoli, pasticiotti*. The only evidence of cleanliness was the magnificent espresso machine at the other end of the counter. It gleamed brightly, all silver and black, polished to a high sheen. Atop it an eagle rampant, its wings spread defiantly, reigned in cast-iron glory.

Louie looked a little sick.

I stirred my coffee. "What's the matter, Louie? Hangover? Or haven't you ever wasted anyone before?"

He nodded bleakly. "No . . . well, no. You know . . ."

I knew, all right. All of a sudden it was no longer so

clean for Uncle Joe's little nephew Louie. All his life he'd been glorying in the Mafia game with all of its excitement, romance, money and mystique. But he had never really been involved himself. For Louie, life had been a good private school, a good college, a good easy job running a legitimate olive oil business, a good time associating with famous mobsters but unsullied by them.

Even his name was clean, I remembered again. "Louie," I asked, "how come your name is Lazaro? Wasn't your Dad named Franzini?"

Louie nodded, smiling ruefully. "Yeah. Luigi Franzini. Lazaro is my mother's maiden name. Uncle Joe had it changed for me when I came to live with him. I guess he wanted to keep me away from all the trouble. I mean, you wouldn't want your kid to be named Al Capone, Jr."

I laughed. "Yeah. Guess you're right. So what are you going to do now?" I asked.

He spread his hands helplessly. "I don't know. It's not like anyone did anything, really. I mean, hell, to just go out and blast a guy because he belongs to the Ruggieros . . ."

It's the facts of life, sonny boy, I thought. I squeezed his shoulder. "You'll think of something, Louie," I said comfortingly.

We stepped out of the Decima and Louie looked up and down the street for a moment, as if trying to make up his mind. "Look, Nick," he said with a sudden grin, "why don't I show you the Counting House?"

"Counting House?"

"Yeah. It's great. The only one of its kind in the world, I'll bet." He took my elbow and led me down the street a few doors. "It's right here, Four fifteen West Broadway."

It didn't look like much. Another one of those big old loft buildings you see in the Soho section of downtown

New York. There was a big blue door over a wide ramp, which I guessed to be the freight elevator. To the right of it was an ordinary residence-type windowed door, with the standard apartment house bank of mailboxes.

Louie led me through the door. Inside the foyer he pushed a button.

A disembodied voice answered. "Yeah? Who is it?"

"Louie Lazaro and a buddy of mine."

"Oh, hi, Louie. C'mon up." A buzzer sounded, long and rasping, and Louie opened the unlocked door. From there, it was five steep flights of narrow stairs. By the time we reached the top, I was having trouble catching my breath and Louie was practically in a state of collapse, his breath coming in gasps and his face dripping sweat.

An amiable looking little man greeted us in the fifth-floor hallway and Louie, in between gasping for breath, introduced me. "This is Nick Canzoneri, Chickie. Chickie Wright, Nick. Chickie runs the Counting House for Uncle Joe. I thought you'd like to see it."

I shrugged. "Sure."

Chickie was a little gnome of a man, with wisps of gray hair floating over his balding head and bushy gray eyebrows sprouting from a humorous little face. He was dressed in a dark blue silk shirt, a black-and-white checked vest, and gray flannel trousers. A bright red bow tie and red garters on his sleeves made him look like a parody of a riverboat gambler. He gave us a huge smile and stood aside to usher us through the big, unmarked blue door that had stood half-opened behind him.

"Come right on in," he said expansively. "This is one of the neatest operations in New York City."

That it was. I hadn't known what to expect of a fifth-floor loft called the Counting House, but it certainly wasn't what I found. Chickie took us through, step by step, explaining the entire operation.

"What we've done," he said with obvious pride, "is computerize our bookie and numbers operations."

The entire loft had been turned into a modern, brightly polished business office. At the front, a huge computer bank whirred and clicked, manned by earnest young men in neat business suits who handled the computerized readouts with consummate familiarity. Attractive secretaries worked attentively along the squarely spaced rows of desks, their electric typewriters competing with each other. The place held all the accoutrements of any executive office building.

Chickie waved an expansive hand. "Every numbers bet made below Houston Street is processed here, and every bet on the horses. All the results from the races come in direct by phone, from Arlington in Chicago all the way east. All the money bet is funnelled through here, all records kept, and all payoffs made from here."

I nodded, impressed. "Electronic data processing comes to bookmaking. Very nice!"

Chickie laughed. "Very efficient. We process around eighty thousand dollars a day here. We figure we have to run it like a business. The days of the little guy in the candy store with a notebook in his hip pocket are over."

"How does the Off-Track Betting affect you?" New York's OTB offices around the city had originally been approved by the voters not only as a way of making money for the city and as a convenience to the bettor, but also as a means of driving out the underworld bookie.

Chickie grinned again. He appeared to be a happy man. "It hasn't hurt us much at all, though I was worried about it once, when it first started. People like to deal with an old established firm, I guess, and they're sort of suspicious of a government running a betting operation.

"And of course, we're heavy into numbers, and the government isn't into the numbers game."

"Not yet, anyway," Louie chimed in. "But the way things are going, they probably will be before long." He clapped me on the shoulder. "What do you think, Nick? Pretty slick, isn't it? Uncle Joe may look and act like an old *Mustachio Pete,* but this has got to be the most modern setup in the business."

Louie's ebullience was exceeded only by his naivete. The Counting House was a step up in underworld organization, but it was hardly the last word. I could show Louie a Mafia-operated communications center in an Indianapolis Hotel that would make New York Telephone look like a PBX switchboard. The results of every gambling event in the country—racing, baseball, basketball, football, you name it—pour into that hotel every day, and then are relayed in microseconds to betting parlors from coast to coast.

Still, the Counting House was an interesting innovation: centralized, organized, efficient. Not bad. "Great," I said. "Terrific!" I tugged at my ear lobe. "I guess you run your trucks business through here, too, huh?"

Louie frowned. "No, but . . . I don't know, it might not be a bad idea at that. Sort of a central command post, you mean?"

"Right."

Chickie looked a little pained. "Well, we really haven't got a lot of room to spare up here, Louie, to say nothing about how hard it is to get someone you can trust these days."

I had to laugh. He was right up to his throat in underworld business but acting like any office manager in any legit concern . . . worried that he might have more work to do, or might have to change his ways of doing it. Honest people aren't the only ones who resist change.

"Nick's new in town," Louie explained, "and I thought I'd show him our showcase operation. Anyway, Uncle Joe's going to have Nick and me going over all the operations one of these days, just to see if we can't tighten things up a bit."

"Yeah." Chickie looked dubious.

"We're mostly going to be worrying about security," I said.

Chickie brightened. "Oh, good. I could use some help there."

"You've been having some trouble?" I asked.

He sighed. "Yeah. More than I want. Come in my office and I'll tell you about it."

We all went into a nicely paneled office in one corner of the big loft. A neat carpet was on the floor, and steel filing cabinets lined all of one wall. A fat safe squatted blackly just behind Chickie's desk. On the desk top were the pictures of an attractive gray-haired woman and a half-dozen children of varying ages.

"Have a seat, guys." Chickie gestured at a couple of straight-back chairs and settled himself into the swivel chair behind the desk. "I got a problem, maybe you can help me with."

Louie hunched his chair up and gave him a confident grin. For the moment, he'd forgotten that Popeye had given him some pretty explicit instructions. Uncle Joe wanted someone killed.

"What's up, Chickie?" Louie asked.

Chickie leaned back and lit a cigarette. "It's Lemon-Drop Droppo, again," he said. "At least I think it's him.

He's been ripping off our runner again. Or at least someone is."

"Hell, Chickie," Louie interjected. "Someone's always ripping off the runners. What's the big deal?"

"The big deal is that it's getting to be a big deal! We got hit fourteen times last week, already five times this week. I can't afford that."

Louie turned to me. "We usually figure three, four times a week we're going to have a runner get taken for whatever he's carrying, but this is a lot more than usual."

"Can't you protect them?" I asked.

Chickie shook his head. "We got a hundred forty-seven guys bringing cash in here every day from all over the lower Manhattan territory. There's no way we can protect 'em all." He grinned. "In fact, I don't even mind if a few of them get ripped off once in awhile, makes the others more careful. But this is getting to be too damned much!"

"What about this Lemon-Drop Droppo?"

Louie laughed. "He's been around a long time, Nick. One of the Ruggiero bunch, but sometimes he goes off sort of independently. He was a runner himself once, for Gaetano Ruggiero, and it seems like every time he's short of cash, he picks on a runner. They're pretty easy pickings, you know."

"Yeah." Runners are at the very bottom of the crime ladder. They pick up the money and the betting slips and run it to the policy bank, and that's it. They're usually half-batty old winos, too far gone down the chute of aged poverty to do anything else, or young kids picking up a fast buck. There are thousands of them in New York, loathsome little ants feeding off the discarded carrion of crime.

"Think it would help if we got rid of this Lemon-Drop character?"

Chickie grinned again. "Couldn't hurt. Even if it's not him, it might scare someone else off."

I nodded and looked at Louie. "Might even kill two birds with one stone, Louie."

This kind of reality didn't come easily to Louie Lazaro. He looked sour. "Yeah," he said.

"How come they call him Lemon-Drop?" I asked.

Louie answered. "He's a nut about lemon drops, eats them all the time. I think his real name is Greggorio, but with a name like Droppo and a bag of lemon drops in his pocket all the time . . . I'd really hate to hit him just for ripping off a few runners. I mean, hell, I went to school with the guy. He's not so bad, just kind of nuts."

I shrugged. I'd been doing a lot of that on this assignment it seemed. "It's up to you. It was just an idea."

Louie looked unhappy. "Yeah. We'll think about it."

"What's this two birds with one stone bit?" Chickie asked.

"Never mind," Louie snapped.

"Yes, sir." Chickie was still very much aware that Louie was Popeye Franzini's nephew.

There was an awkward pause. I waved a hand at the row of gleaming file cabinets, each stack locked with a formidable looking iron rod running from the floor up through each drawer handle and bolted to the top of the file. "What you got in there, the family jewels?"

Chickie stubbed out his cigarette and grinned, glad of the change of atmosphere. "Those are our files," he said. "Records of the whole thing from A to Z."

"Everything?" I tried to sound impressed. "You mean for the whole betting operation?"

"I mean for the whole organization," he said. "Everything."

I looked around. "How good is your security?"

"Fine. Fine. That part of it I'm not worried about. We're on the fifth floor here. The other four floors are empty except for a couple of apartments we use in emergencies. Every night we put steel gates across each landing. They fit right into the wall and lock there. And then there's the dogs," he added pridefully.

"The dogs?"

"Yeah. On each floor we got two guard dogs, Doberman Pinschers. We let 'em loose each night, two on each floor. I mean, man, there ain't nobody's gonna come up those stairs with those dogs. They're mean sons of bitches! Even without them, there's no way anyone's going to blast through those gates without alerting Big Julie and Raymond."

"Who're they?"

"My two guards. They live up here every night. Once everyone leaves and they lock those gates, there's no way anyone could get in."

"Looks good to me," I said. "If Big Julie and Raymond can take care of themselves."

Chickie laughed. "Don't worry, man. Big Julie's the strongest guy this side of the circus and Raymond used to be one of the best ordnance sergeants in Korea. He knows what guns are all about."

"Good enough for me." I got to my feet and Louie did the same. "Thanks a lot, Chickie," I said. "We'll be seeing you, I guess."

"Right," he said. We shook hands, and Louie and I went back down the staircase. Alerted now, I could see the steel gates inset into the walls on each landing. It was a nice tight setup, but I had an idea how it might be breached.

CHAPTER 13

Dinner was delightful, a small table in the back of Minetta's, on a night when there was hardly anyone there—a light antipasto, a good oso buco, zuccini strips fried in deep fat, and espresso coffee. Philomina was in that loving, glowing mood that puts a little excitement in life.

It all turned into a petulant Siciliano rage when I kissed her goodnight in front of her door. She stamped her foot, accused me of going to bed with six other girls, burst into tears, and finally ended up throwing her arms around my neck and smothering me with kisses.

"Nick . . . please, Nick. Just for a little while."

I disentangled myself firmly. I knew that if I went in, I'd be there much too long. I had things to do that night. I kissed her firmly on the end of her nose, spun her around so that she faced her own door, and smacked her smartly on her round behind. "Go on. Just leave the door ajar and I'll see you when I get through with the things I have to take care of."

Her smile was all-forgiving and, happy again, she said, "Promise?"

"Promise." I went back down the hall before my resolve weakened.

The first thing I did when I got to my room at the Chelsea was call Louie. "Hi, this is Nick. Look, how about meeting me tonight? Yeah, I know it's late, but it's important. Right! Oh, about midnight. And bring Locallo and Manitta. At Tony's, I guess. It's as good as any. Okay? Good . . . oh, and Louie, get hold of Lemon-Drop Droppo's address before you come, will you?"

I hung up before he could react to that last request. Then I went downstairs and around the corner to the Angry Squire. I ordered a mug of beer from Sally, the congenial English Barmaid, and then made a call to Washington from the phone on the wall at the end of the bar. It was just a routine precaution in case my hotel room phone was bugged.

I called AXE's Emergency Supply Section and, after identifying myself properly, orderd a 17B Demolition Kit sent to me that night by Greyhound Bus. I would be able to pick it up in the morning at the Port Authority bus terminal on Eighth Avenue.

The 17B Kit is very neat, very destructive. Six detonator caps, six timer fuses that can be set to trigger the caps at any interval between one minute and fifteen hours, six pieces of primer cord for less sophisticated jobs, and enough plastique to blow the crown off the Statue of Liberty's head.

It was difficult to make myself understood over the din created by a very good but very loud jazz combo some six feet away, but I finally got my message across and hung up.

At eleven-thirty I left the Angry Squire and wandered

down Seventh Avenue, making plans for Lemon-Drop Droppo. At the corner of Christopher and Seventh, I turned right on Christopher past all the new gay bars, then turned left again on Bedford Street and down the short block and a half to Tony's.

It was an entirely different scene from what it had been just the night before at Philomina's party. Now it was quiet and intimate again, back to its usual dungeon-like ambiance, the dull orange lights on the dark brown walls casting barely enough light to allow the waiters to maneuver between the tables that were back in their accustomed places in the main room.

In place of the hordes of tuxedo-clad Italian hoods and their long-gowned women, the place was now sparsely populated with a half-dozen long-haired young guys in blue jeans and denim jackets and an equal number of short-haired young girls similarly clad. But the conversation wasn't much different from the previous evening. Where the talk at the party had centered primarily on sex, football games, and horses, tonight's crowd talked mostly of sex, football games, and philosophy.

Louie was at a table by himself, up against the wall to the left of the entrance, hunched morosely over a glass of wine. He didn't look too happy.

I sat down with him, ordered a brandy and soda and clapped him on the shoulder. "Come on, Louie, cheer up. Things aren't as bad as all that!"

He tried a grin but it didn't come off.

"Louie, you really don't want to do it, do you?"

"Do what?"

Who was he kidding? "Take care of Droppo."

He shook his head miserably, not meeting my eyes. "No, I mean, it's just that . . . oh, hell! No!" he said with more force, glad to get it out in the open. "No! I don't want to do it. I don't think I *can* do it. I just . . . hell, I grew up with the guy, Nick!"

"Okay! Okay! I think I've got an idea that will take care of the Lemon Drop kid, make your Uncle Joe happy, and get you off the hook. How's that for a package?"

Hope gleamed in his eyes and that delightful smile of his began to spread across his face. "Honest? Hey, Nick, that would be great!"

"Okay. You did me a favor in Beirut, getting me over here. Now I do you one, right?"

He nodded.

"All right. First, I got this in my box at the Chelsea today." I handed him a note I had written myself.

> Canzoneri: You'll find Spelman
> In Room 636 Chalfont Plaza Hotel.
> He's bare-assed and dead as hell.

Louie stared at it in disbelief. "Jeez! What the hell is this all about? Do you suppose it's true?"

"It's probably true, all right. There wouldn't be any sense in sending that to me if it weren't."

"No, I guess not. But why the hell would they send it? You just got here!"

I shrugged. "Beats the hell out of me. The room clerk just said some guy came by and left it. Maybe whoever it was figured I was just handy and would pass it on to you anyway."

Louie looked puzzled, as he should have. "I still don't get it." He paused a minute, thinking. "Listen, Nick. Do you suppose it was the Ruggieros?"

Atta baby, Louie! I thought. "Yeah," I said. "That's what I figure."

He frowned. "So what's this got to do with coming down here tonight? And with Lemon-Drop Droppo?"

"Just an idea. You got Locallo and Manitti with you?"

"Yeah. They're out in the car."

"Good. Now here's what we're going to do." I explained my idea to him, and he was delighted.

"Great, Nick! Great!"

It was only a few blocks over to 88 Horatio, which is just about a block or so off Hudson. I explained to Locallo and Manitti as we drove over. "Remember. We want him alive. It's all right if he's a little damaged, but I don't want any bodies. Understand?"

Locallo, behind the wheel, shrugged. "It sounds crazy to me."

Louie punched him lightly on the back of the head to let him know who was boss. "No one asked you. Just do like Nick says."

Eighty-eight Horatio was a faceless gray building with a line of identical high-stepped front stoops and iron railings. It took Manitti something like forty-five seconds to get through the lock on the outside door and another thirty to open the inside one. We filed up the stairway as quietly as possible, pausing finally on the sixth-floor landing to stop panting from the climb. There were just three of us—Locallo, Manitti and myself—since we had left Louie downstairs in the car.

Manitti had no trouble with the apartment door to 6B. He didn't use a plastic card like they do in all the espionage books these days. He just used an old-fashioned flat blade shaped much like a surgeon's scalpel and a small tool that looked something like a steel knitting needle. It didn't take more than twenty seconds before the door swung open silently, and Manitti stepped aside to let me enter, a big congratulatory smile of self-satisfaction on his Neanderthal face.

There were no lights on in what was obviously a living room, but a light did shine beneath a closed door across the room. I moved across quickly, Locallo and Manitti right behind, each of us with a gun in hand.

I reached the door, flung it open, and stepped into the bedroom in one quick motion. I didn't want to give Droppo a chance to go for a gun.

I needn't have bothered.

Greggorio Droppo was much too busy, at least for the moment, to worry about such a small incident as three armed men bursting into his bedroom at one o'clock in the morning. Droppo's naked body heaved spasmodically, twisting and churning the sheets under the girl he was making love to. Her arms were tight around his neck, pulling him to her, their faces locked together so that all we could see was grease-slicked hair, mussed now by the grasping fingers of the girl. Her slender legs, shapely and white against the hairy darkness of his body, were scissored around his waist, locked against the slipperiness of the sweat that poured from him. Her arms and legs were all we could see of her.

With a great threshing effort, Droppo reared backward and upward, the classic stud movement before the final screaming plunge. Not having a glass of ice water handy, I did the next best thing and kicked him in the ribs with the point of my shoe.

He froze. Then his head snapped around, eyes wide in disbelief. "Wha-a-a-at . . . ?"

I kicked him again and he gasped in pain. He pulled out, rolling off the girl and onto his back, holding his side in agony.

The sudden departure of her lover left the girl spread-eagled on her back, eyes protruding in terror. She half-raised herself on her elbows, her mouth opened to scream. I clasped my left hand over her mouth and forced her flat back against the sheets, then leaned over and pointed Wilhelmina at her, the muzzle just an inch from her eyes.

She struggled for a moment, arching her sweaty body under the pressure of my hand, then realized what she was looking at and froze, her gaze riveted on the gun. Beads of perspiration stood out on her forehead, matting the disheveled strands of her red hair.

Next to her, Droppo started to swing his legs over the side of the bed but Locallo was there. Almost casually he whipped the barrel of his revolver across Droppo's face and he dropped back with an anguished howl, clutching at his bloody nose. With one hand, Locallo whipped a crumpled pillow up off the floor and crammed it over Droppo's face, shutting off the sounds. With the other, he smashed between Droppo's extended legs so that the butt of his pistol slammed into the naked man's groin.

An animal sound came from beneath the pillow and the body convulsed high into the air, back arched, all the weight on the shoulders, then collapsed limply on the bed.

"He's passed out, boss," Locallo said laconically. I think he was disappointed.

"Take the pillow away so he doesn't suffocate," I ordered. I looked down at the girl and waved Wilhelmina menacingly. "No noise, no nothing when I take my hand away. Understand?"

She nodded as best she could, eyes staring at me in terror. "Okay," I said. "Relax. We're not going to hurt you." I took my hand away from her mouth and stepped back.

She lay motionless, and the three of us stood there, guns in hand, taking in her beauty. Even with the sweat of sex on her, the terror in her eyes, and the tangled mass of hair, she was exquisite. Her bare breasts heaved and tears suddenly poured from the green eyes.

"Please, please don't hurt me," she whimpered. "Please, Nick."

Then I recognized her. It was Rusty Pollard, the little redhead in the green dress I'd flirted with at the party at Tony's, the same one who, years before, had begun Philomina's torment with an anonymous envelope containing a clipping from the *Times*.

Standing next to me, Manitti was beginning to breathe hard. "Son of a bitch!" he exclaimed. He leaned over the bed, one hand reaching for her breast.

I cracked him across the side of the head with my gun hand and he jerked back, stunned.

Tears streamed down Rusty's cheeks. I looked at her naked body contemptuously. "If it's not one little squat Italian, it's another, right, Rusty?"

She gulped, but didn't answer.

I reached over and prodded Droppo, but he was inert. "Bring him to," I told Locallo.

I turned back to Rusty. "Get up and get dressed."

She started to sit up slowly and looked at her own naked body as if just realizing that she was lying completely nude in a room with four men, three of whom were virtual strangers.

She jerked into a sitting position, snapping her knees together and doubling them up in front of her. She crossed her arms over her breasts and glared at us wildly. "You lousy sons of bitches," she spat.

I laughed. "Don't be so modest, Rusty. We've already seen you making it with this jerk. We're not likely to see you looking any worse." I yanked her by the arm and pulled her out of bed onto the floor.

I could feel that one little spark of fight go out of her right there. I let go and she slowly got to her feet and went over to the chair next to the bed, avoiding our eyes. She picked up a lacy black bra and started to put it on, looking away at the wall as she did. Complete humiliation.

Manitti licked his lips and I glared at him. Locallo came back from the kitchen carrying four cans of cold beer.

He put them all down on the dresser and opened them carefully. He gave one to me, one to Manitti, and took one himself. Then he took the fourth one and poured it steadily over the inert body of Lemon-Drop Droppo, the beer slopping over the sweaty form and soaking the sheet around him.

Droppo came to with a groan, hands instinctively reaching for his outraged genitals.

I tapped him on the bridge of his mangled nose with Wilhelmina just hard enough to make tears start in his eyes. "Who?" he gasped, "what . . . ?"

"Just do exactly what I say, chum, and you might survive."

"Who?" he managed to get out again.

I smiled benignly. "Popeye Franzini," I said. "Now get up and get dressed."

Terror showed in his eyes as he slowly rose from the bed, one hand still clutching his groin. He dressed slowly, and gradually I could sense a change in his attitude. He was trying to appraise the situation, looking for a way out. He was hating more than hurting, and a hating man is dangerous.

Droppo finished the laborious process of tying his shoes, an occasional groan escaping his tightly compressed lips, then used both hands on the bed to lever himself to his feet. As soon as he was standing I slammed my knee into his crotch. He screamed and crumpled to the floor in a dead faint.

I motioned to Locallo. "Get him up again, Franco."

On the other side of the room, fully dressed now, Rusty Pollard suddenly came alive again. Her hair was still mused and her lipstick smeared, but the kelly green skirt and black silk blouse she had put on over her bra and panties had given her courage again.

"That was brutal," she hissed. "He wasn't doing anything to you."

"Sending that clipping to Philomina Franzini years ago was brutal, too," I retorted. "She wasn't doing anything to you, either."

The last bit of brutalizing had taken the final vestige of fighting spirit out of Lemon-Drop Droppo and he came down the stairs with us quietly, slightly bent over, both hands pressed tightly to his abdomen.

We put Rusty up front with Locallo and Manitti, and jammed Droppo between Louie and me in the back seat. Then we drove to the Chalfont Plaza. Louie, Droppo, and I went in the main entrance of Manny's place while the other three went in through the Lexington Avenue side.

We met in front of Room 636. I took the Do Not Disturb sign off the door and turned the key. The smell wasn't too bad since I had turned the air conditioner on full blast before leaving two nights before, but it was noticeable.

"What's that smell?" Rusty asked, trying to pull back. I gave her a hard shove that sent her sprawling halfway across the room and we all went in. Manitti closed the door behind us.

I had warned the others what to expect and Droppo was in too much pain to really care. Not Rusty, though.

She got to her feet with a look of sheer viciousness. "What the hell is going on here?" she screeched. "What's that smell?"

I opened the bathroom door and showed her Larry Spelman's naked body.

"Oh my God! Oh my God!" Rusty wailed, hiding her face in her hands.

"Now take off your clothes, both of you," I ordered.

Droppo, his face still drawn with pain, began dumbly to comply. He was past asking questions.

Not Rusty. "What are you going to do?" she screamed at me. "My God . . ."

"Forget God," I snapped, "and get undressed. Or do you want me to have Gino do it for you?"

Manitti leered at her, and slowly Rusty began unbuttoning her blouse. Stripped down to her bra and bikini panties, she hesitated again, but I waved Wilhelmina at her and she finished the job defiantly, throwing her clothes in a little heap on the floor.

Louie picked up both sets of clothing and stuffed them into a small bag he had brought along. Droppo sat on the edge of the bed, staring at the floor. Rusty was backed in a corner by the dresser, half-turned so that all we could see was her bare hip. Her arms covered her breasts and she shivered a bit. The room was cold from the air conditioning.

I paused at the doorway as we went out. "Now I want you two lovebirds to stay right here," I said. "Somebody will be up in a little while and you can get everything straightened out. In the meantime, Manitti here is going to be standing right outside the door. If it so much as opens one little crack before anyone else gets here, he'll kill you. Do you understand that?" I paused. "At least he'll kill you, Droppo. I don't know what he'll do to Rusty."

I closed the door and we all went down on the elevator.

In the lobby, I used a pay phone to call Jack Gourlay.

"Son of a bitch!" he grumbled over the phone. "It's two o'clock in the morning."

"Forget it," I said. "I've got a story for you in Room 636 at the Chalfont Plaza."

"It had better be good."

"Well," I drawled. "Sounds pretty good to me, Jack. There's three people up there in Room 636, they're all naked and one of them is dead. And one of them is female."

"Jesus Christ!" There was a long pause. "Mafia?"

"Mafia," I said, and hung up.

We all went across the street to the Sunrise Cocktail Lounge and had a drink. Then we went home.

CHAPTER 14

Philomina removed my hand from her left breast and sat upright in bed, squishing the pillow up behind her so it supported the small of her back. She frowned perplexedly.

"But I don't understand, Nick. It's kind of funny, or awful, or something. The police won't be able to prove that Rusty and Droppo killed Larry Spelman, will they? I mean . . ."

I kissed her right breast and squirmed around so I could rest my head on her stomach, lying crosswise across the bed.

I explained. "They're not going to be able to prove that Rusty and Droppo killed Spelman, but those two are going to have one hell of a time for awhile trying to prove that they *didn't*."

"You mean the cops will just let them go?"

"Not quite. Remember, I told you I left that metal cigar container on the dresser before I left?"

She nodded.

"It was full of heroin. They'll both get busted for possession."

"Oh." She frowned. "I hope Rusty doesn't have to go to jail. I mean, I hate her, but . . ."

I patted her knee, which was somewhere to the left of my left ear. "Don't worry. There'll be a lot of stuff in the newspapers, and a lot of people scratching heads, but it's such a screwy setup, any good lawyer will be able to get them off."

"I still don't understand it," she said. "Won't the police be looking for you and Louie?"

"Not a chance. Droppo *knows*, but he's not about to *tell* the cops what happened. It's too damned humiliating. He'll never admit to them that a rival gang could get away with that. The Ruggieros are going to be pretty pissed off, on the other hand, and that's just what we want."

"What will they do?"

"Well, if they react like I hope they will, they'll come out shooting."

The papers certainly came out shooting the next day. Give a newspaperman a nude man and a nude girl in a hotel room with a nude corpse and he's going to be happy. Add two rival underworld factions and a container of high-grade heroin and he's going to be ecstatic. Jack Gourlay was in journalistic seventh heaven.

The pictures in the *News* the next morning were as good as I've ever seen. The photographer had caught Droppo sitting naked on the bed with Rusty naked in the background, trying to shield herself with crossed arms. They had had to do a little air-brushing to make it decent enough to print. The headline writer had had a good time too:

NUDE MAFIOSO AND GAL CAUGHT
BAREHANDED WITH CORPSE AND DOPE

The New York Times did not consider it a front-page story, as the *News* had, but it rated a six-column binder on page sixteen with a column and a half of type and a sidebar about the history of the Mafia in New York. Both Franzini and the Ruggieros got a big play, including a fairly detailed account of Popeye's alleged set-to with Philomina's father years before.

Popeye himself couldn't have cared less. He was delighted to the extent that his hatred of the world would let him be. He roared with laughter when Louie showed him the story the next day, leaning back in his wheelchair and howling. The fact that Larry Spelman had been killed didn't bother him in the slightest, apparently, except as Spelman's death reflected an insult by the Ruggieros to the Franzinis.

As far as Popeye was concerned, the embarrassment and loss of dignity suffered by the Ruggieros through having one of their button men caught in such a ridiculous situation more than made up for murder. With the Franzinis of this world, murder is commonplace, absurdity a rarity.

Louie was delighted, too, with the new stature he had gained in his uncle's eyes. I didn't have to give him all the credit. By the time I got to the offices of Franzini Olive Oil that morning, Louie was already basking in praise. I'm sure Louie didn't actually tell Popeye that it was his idea, but he didn't tell him it wasn't, either.

I sat back and waited for the Ruggieros to retaliate.

Nothing happened, and I re-examined my position. I had apparently underestimated Ruggiero. Thinking back, I had to realize that Gaetano Ruggiero was not the type of leader who could be panicked into a bloody and expensive gang war by the kind of shenanigans I had been up to.

Popeye Franzini might be easily provoked, but not Ruggiero. This being the case, I picked on Popeye again. I could depend upon him to react, and react violently. I'd had a plan earlier, which was why I had ordered that 17B kit from Washington, and I just needed a little help from Philomina to put it into operation. My target was the Counting House, the heart of the entire Franzini operation.

I hit it just five days after the Lemon-Drop Droppo caper.

All I needed from Philomina was an alibi in case one of the guards at the Counting House could identify me later. I intended to make sure that they couldn't, but it was an easy enough precaution to take.

It was an open secret around Franzini Olive Oil Co. that Philomina was "seein' a lotta that new guy, Nick, the guy Louie brought back from over there." It was simple. We just made a big deal of going to a David Amram concert that night at Lincoln Center. It's almost impossible to get tickets to an Amram concert in New York these days, so it was natural we should brag a bit about the ones I had gotten. Only no one knew they were from Jack Gourlay at the *News*.

I waited until the house lights went down, then left. Amram may be the finest contemporary composer in America, but I had a lot of work to do, and not much time to do it in. I wanted to be back before the performance ended.

It took less than fifteen minutes to take a cab from Lincoln Center down to Soho, 417 West Broadway, next to the Counting House.

It was a similar building, four floors of apartments with a big loft on the upper floor. It lacked the freight elevator that marked the building next door, but it also lacked those guard dogs on each floor, to say nothing of the steel gratings on each landing. There was no way I was going to try going up the stairway in the Counting House. It's virtually impossible to pick the lock of a steel grating with one hand while fighting off a blood-mad Doberman Pinscher with the other.

I entered the building at 417 and scanned the names next to the doorbell buzzers. I picked one at random—Candy Gulko—and rang the bell.

A moment went by before a voice issued from the built-in speaker. "Yes?"

It was a woman's voice, happily. "Fremonti Flower Shop," I answered.

Pause. "What?"

I added a touch of impatience to my tone. "Fremonti Flower Shop, ma'am. I've got some flowers for Candy Gulko."

"Oh! Come right on up." The buzzer went off, releasing the automatic lock on the inner doorway, and I went in and upstairs, swinging my brand new attaché case like any solid New York businessman.

I didn't stop at Candy Gulko's floor, of course. Instead, I climbed straight up, past the fifth floor, and up the last small flight of stairs that led onto the roof.

It was only a matter of minutes before I was crouched on the roof of 417 West Broadway, contemplating the ten feet of open air between the two buildings, and my imagination plummeted to the ground with no difficulty.

I looked around the tar-papered roof and, lying against

a brick chimney, finally found what I wanted, a long narrow plank. I wished it wasn't so narrow, but there was no hope for it. I had to have a bridge. When I was in college I broadjumped twenty-four-feet six-inches, but that was a long time ago, it was in daylight, with a good runway, spike shoes and—most importantly—on ground level. I wasn't about to try jumping those ten feet between buildings that night.

The plank was only about six inches wide, wide enough for purchase but too narrow for confidence. I pushed it across the gap between the two buildings so that it rested equally on each roof. Holding my attaché case in both hands in front of me, I placed one tentative foot on my shaky bridge, braced myself, and ran across in three steps.

I had to run. I don't normally suffer from acrophobia but if I'd tried to edge my way across, I would never have made it. Fear would have forced me into a misstep, and there was no room for a misstep. I stood stiffly for several minutes, composing myself, still trembling but sweating with relief.

Once I had calmed myself, I went over to the doorway leading to the staircase. If it were bolted from the inside, I would have to get into the Counting House offices through the skylight, and that would be difficult.

The door was unlocked. I had merely to open it and push my way through. It was somewhat like the British had done at Singapore: All their guns pointed to sea to stave off any naval attack; the Japanese took the overland route, came in the "back door" and captured Singapore. Similarly, the Counting House's defenses were all geared to preventing entrance from below; they had never considered that a raid might come from above.

I thought about knocking at the door of the Counting House office on the fifth floor just to give Big Julie and

Raymond something to think about in their barricaded little nest, but I couldn't afford to alert them just to please my own perverse sense of humor.

I slipped a black nylon stocking over my face, opened the door and walked in, my attaché case in one hand, Wilhelmina in the other.

Two men stared at me, paralyzed by surprise. They were sitting on either side of a steel-topped deşk, on which they had been playing cards. A half-empty bottle of gin stood on the desktop along with two glasses and a couple of overflowing ashtrays. To one side the remains of a sandwich rested on a brown paper bag. Smoke hung in the air under the low-hanging desk light. In the shadows around the huge room, a great computer stood silent guard over the rows of motionless desks and silent typewriters.

A few feet away from the desk, two old-style army cots had been set up, side by side.

One of the men at the desk was huge, his great muscled body gleaming in the light. He was wearing a sleeveless undershirt with a pair of ratty looking gray slacks hooked loosely under his spreading paunch. The butt of a fat cigar was clamped in yellowed teeth beneath a great bush of a mustache. Big Julie, no doubt.

His companion was more average in size, a real street dude with a wide-brimmed green felt hat, a bright red silk shirt open almost to the waist, and flaring trousers in an Aqueduct plaid. Two oversized diamond rings gleamed on Raymond's left hand, contrasting with the blackness of his skin. He surprised me. I hadn't expected that one of Chickie Wright's boys would be black. If the lower-class Italian with the big-time ideas was finally beginning to lose his innate prejudices, the world was indeed becoming a better place to live in.

The paralysis of surprise lasted only a moment. Raymond's left hand suddenly flashed toward the shoulder holster hanging over the back of a typist's chair next to him.

Wilhelmina barked and a bullet slammed into the chair, jerking it backward a few inches. Raymond's hand froze in midair, then slowly returned to the table.

"Thank you," I said politely. "Just remain right where you are, gentlemen."

Big Julie's eyes bulged and the cigar stub moved spasmodically in the corner of his mouth. "What the hell . . ." he croaked in a guttural voice.

"Shut up." I waved Wilhelmina at him, keeping a close eye on Raymond. Of the two, I had decided that he was the more dangerous. I was wrong, but I didn't know it at the time.

I laid my attaché case on a neat desk in front of me and opened it with my left hand. I took out two long pieces of rawhide I'd picked up that afternoon at a shoe repair shop.

Somewhere downstairs a dog barked.

The two guards looked at each other, then back at me.

"The dogs," Big Julie croaked. "How'd'ja get by the dogs?"

I grinned. "Just petted them on the head as I went by. I love dogs."

He grunted in disbelief. "The gates . . . ?"

I grinned again. "I burned them down with my super ray gun." I took a step closer and waved the gun again. "You. Raymond. Lie down on the floor on your face."

"Screw you, man!"

I fired. The shot hit the top of the desk and ricocheted. It's hard to tell where a bullet bounces, but from the mark it put on the desktop it must have missed Raymond's nose by millimeters.

He reared back in his chair, hands high above his head. "Yes, sir. On the floor. Right away." He got slowly to his feet, hands held high, then lowered himself gingerly to the floor, face down.

"Put your hands behind your back."

He obeyed instantly.

Next I turned to Julie, and had to laugh. He still held the deck of cards in his hand. He must have been dealing when I came in.

"Okay," I said, tossing him one of the rawhide thongs. "Tie your buddy up."

He stared down at the thong, then up at me. Finally he laid down the cards and got clumsily to his feet. He picked up the thong dumbly and stood looking at it.

"Move it! Tie his hands behind his back."

Big Julie did as he was told. When he was through and had stepped back, I checked the knots. He'd done a good enough job.

I waved the pistol at him again. "Okay. Now it's your turn. On the floor."

"What the . . ."

"I said on the floor!"

He sighed, carefully removed the cigar butt from his mouth, and laid it in the ashtray on the desk. Then he lay down on the floor, several feet away from Raymond.

"Put your hands behind your back."

He sighed again and put his hands behind his back, his cheek flat against the floor.

I laid Wilhelmina on the chair Big Julie had been sitting on and knelt over him, straddling his body to tie his hands.

His feet whipped up, cracking into my back, and his

giant body twisted and heaved in a great convulsion of effort, throwing me against the desk and off balance. I cursed my own stupidity and dove for the gun, but he caught my wrist in a viselike grip with one beefy paw, heaving over against me with his body and pinning me to the floor with his great weight.

His face was next to mine, pressing against me. He raised back and smashed downward with his head, trying to crack it against mine. I twisted violently and his head cracked against the floor. He bellowed like a stuck bull and twisted over on me again.

I clawed at his eyes with my free hand, fighting against the weight pressing down on me, arching my back to keep my body from being flattened helplessly under him. My searching fingers found his eyes, but they were squinted tightly shut. I took the next best alternative, jamming two fingers into his nostrils and ripping back and upward.

I could feel tissue give, and he screamed, letting go of my other wrist so that he could pull on the attacking hand. I pushed off with my free hand and we rolled over and over on the floor. We came up against the leg of a desk. I grabbed both of his ears and pounded his head backward against the metal furniture.

His grip slackened and I broke free, tumbling away from him. I snapped to my feet just in time to see Raymond, hands still tied behind him, struggling to stand. I kicked him in the stomach with the point of my shoe and dove to retrieve Wilhelmina from where I'd left her on the chair.

I grabbed the Luger and spun just as Big Julie launched himself from the floor at me like a grunting, sweating catapult. I sidestepped and let him hurtle by me as I smashed at the side of his head with the butt of the pistol. He crashed headlong into the chair and lay there, suddenly inert, blood from his ripped nose spreading over his lower jaw, soaking his mustache. On the floor alongside him, Raymond squirmed and moaned, hands still locked behind his back.

I reholstered Wilhelmina. It had been such a clean operation until Big Julie had gone heroic on me. I waited until I was breathing normally, then tied Big Julie's hands together as I had started to do a few minutes before. Then I turned on all the lights in the office and began going through the big bank of files in Chickie Wright's office.

They were locked but it didn't take me long to break the locks. Finding what I was looking for, however, was a different matter. But finally I found it. A dollar-by-dollar breakdown of the Franzini holdings in the city's business concerns.

I whistled. Popeye was not only into everything illegal in the city, he hadn't missed many legal operations: meatpacking, stock brokerage, construction, taxicabs, hotels, electrical appliances, pasta manufacturing, supermarkets, bakeries, massage parlors, movie houses, pharmaceutical manufacturing.

I pulled open one of the file drawers and noticed some large manila envelopes piled in the back. They had no labels and the flaps were sealed. I ripped them open and knew I'd hit the jackpot. Those envelopes contained the records—with sale dates, drops, names, everything—of Franzini's heroin operation, a complex pipeline from the Middle East to New York.

It seemed my late friend, Su Lao Lin, hadn't gone out of the drug business when our GI's left Indochina. She'd just moved shop a few thousand miles to Beirut. That beautiful woman was funneling drugs as well as men. She was a busy girl.

Her relationship to Franzini always had puzzled me. It

had always nagged at the back of my mind why I'd met a
Red Chinese agent and former drug distributor working as
an employment service for an American gangster. She was
just doing double duty and I'd been involved in only one
side of her many talents for organization. It all became
clear, and I smiled slightly as I thought that I'd inadvertently blown up Franzini's Middle Eastern connection.

Whatever misgivings I'd had earlier about wiping her
out were completely gone.

I stacked the papers carefully on the desk next to my
attaché case and then took the plastique explosives out of
the case and lined them up. Plastique is not too stable,
and it should be handled carefully. When I had it sent to
me by bus from Washington, I'd had it sent in two pack-
ages—one for the explosive itself, the other for the caps
and detonators. That way, it was safe.

Now, I carefully went about inserting the caps and the
timer-detonators. Set for maximum, the detonators would
go off in five minutes once they had been activated.
I placed one where it was sure to destroy the computer,
then distributed the other three around the room where
they would do maximum damage. I didn't have to be too
precise. Four plastique bombs would pretty well demolish
the Counting House.

"Man, you ain't gonna leave us here." It was more a
plea than a question from the black man on the floor. He
had twisted around so that he could watch me. He had
quit groaning some time ago.

I smiled down at him. "No, Raymond. You and your
fat friend are going with me." I looked over at Big Julie,
who had raised himself into a sitting position on the floor
and was glaring at me through bloodshot eyes. "I want
someone to carry a message for me to Popeye Franzini."

"What's the message?" Raymond was eager to oblige.

"Just tell him that tonight's work was with the compliments of Gaetano Ruggiero."

"Well, goddamn . . ." It was Big Julie. Blood streamed down his face from his torn nose.

I repacked my attaché case carefully, making sure all the incriminating papers were in it, then closed and locked it. I got Raymond and Big Julie to their feet and made them stand in the middle of the room while I went around and activated the timing devices on each of the detonators. Then the three of us got out of there in a hurry, rushing up the stairway to the roof and slamming the rooftop door shut behind us.

I made Raymond and Big Julie lie down on their faces again, then took a deep breath and dashed across my shaky plank bridge to the next building. Once across, I pulled the plank aside, tossed it onto the rooftop and started down the stairway, whistling happily to myself. It had been a good night's work.

Halfway down the stairs I could feel the building shake as four big explosions sounded from next door. When I got outside, the top floor of 415 West Broadway was in flames. I stopped on the corner to pull the fire alarm box, then strolled on over to Sixth Avenue and hailed a cab going uptown. I was back in my seat alongside Philomina before the end of the Amram concerto that was the finale on the program.

My clothes were slightly mussed, but I had brushed off most of the dirt I'd picked up rolling around on the floor of the Counting House. The informal way some people dress for concerts these days, it wouldn't be very noticeable.

CHAPTER 15

After Philomina had gone to work the next morning, I wrapped up the papers I had taken from the Counting House and mailed them to Ron Brandenburg. There was enough there to keep the FBI, the Treasury Department, and the Southern District Task Force Against Organized Crime busy for the next six months.

Then I called Washington and ordered another 17B Explosive Kit. I was beginning to feel like the Mad Bomber, but you can't take on the Mafia alone with only a pistol and a stiletto.

When I finally got myself organized, I called Louie.

He practically jumped over the telephone line at me. "Jeez, Nick, am I glad you called! The whole goddamned place has gone nuts! You gotta get over here right away. We've . . ."

"Slow down, slow down. What's going on?"

"Everything!"

"Take it easy, Louie. Take it easy. What's happening, for Chrissake?"

He was so excited he had a hard time telling me, but it eventually came out.

Someone from Ruggiero's mob had blown up the Counting House, the firemen had just barely made it in time to rescue the two guards, who'd been beaten up, bound, and left to die on the rooftop.

Left to die, hell! But I didn't say anything.

Popeye Franzini, Louie went on, was in an enraged frenzy, screaming and pounding his desk between periods of morose depression when he just sat in his wheelchair and stared out the window. The destruction of the Counting House was the last straw, Louie babbled. The Franzini gang was "going to the mattresses"—in Mafia terms, setting up bare apartments around town, where six to ten "soldiers" could hole up, away from their usual haunts, protected by each other. The apartments, equipped with extra mattresses for those Mafioso staying in them, not only served as "safe houses," but as bases from which the buttonmen could strike out at the opposing force.

It was the beginning of the biggest gang war in New York since the Gallos and Colombos had fought it out in a battle that ended with Colombo paralyzed and Gallo dead.

Louie, myself, Locallo and Manitti went to the mattresses with a half-dozen other Franzini hoods in a third-floor walkup apartment on Houston Street. It had three windows giving a good view of the street and—once I had secured the rooftop door—only one means of access—up the narrow stairs.

We moved in, sat down, and waited for the next move. A few blocks up the street, the Ruggieros did the same. We had a half-dozen other apartments similarly occupied and so did our rivals: Each with a half-dozen or more hard cases, each with a full supply of pistols, rifles, submachine guns, and ammunition, each with its local messenger boy to bring in the papers and fresh beer and take-out orders of food, each with its 24-hour-a-day poker game, each with its endless television, each with its intolerable boredom.

Philomina was on the phone three times a day, to the extent that she prompted a few obscene remarks out of one of Louie's hood friends. I knocked out two of his teeth and no one commented after that.

It was Philomina, and the newspapers brought in daily by our messenger, that kept us up with the outside world. Actually, nothing much was going on. According to Philomina, the word was that Gaetano Ruggiero was insisting he had had nothing to do with either Spelman's death or the explosions at the Counting House. He kept passing the word that he wanted to negotiate, but Popeye was playing it cool. The last time Ruggiero had been known to negotiate, in the hassle a few years back with the San Remos, it had been a trap that ended up with the San Remos being killed.

On the other hand, according to Philomina, Popeye figured that if Ruggiero *did* want to negotiate, then he didn't want to antagonize his rival any further. So for two weeks, both factions hung around in those dreary apartments, jumping at imagined shadows.

Even Italian hoods can get bored after a while. We weren't supposed to leave the apartment for any reason, but I had to speak to Philomina without the others around. One night, the other guys approved of the idea of some more cold beer—my suggestion—and I volunteered to go out for it. I managed to override the others' warnings of Franzini's wrath and the danger I was letting myself in for, and they finally agreed, believing I was the most stir-crazy of the bunch.

On my way back from a nearby delicatessen, I called Philomina.

"I think Uncle Joe is getting ready to meet with Mr. Ruggiero," she told me.

I couldn't afford that. Half my battle plan was to set one mob against the other, to get things to such a fever pitch that the Commission would have to step in.

I thought a moment. "All right. Now listen carefully. Have Jack Gourlay call the apartment in about ten minutes and ask for Louie." Then I outlined in detail for her what I wanted Jack to tell Louie.

The phone rang about five minutes after I got back and Louie took it.

"Yeah? No kidding? Sure . . . Sure . . . Okay . . . Yeah, sure . . . Right away . . . ? Okay."

He hung up with an excited look on his face. Self-consciously, he pushed at the big .45 strapped to his chest in a shoulder holster. "It's one of Uncle Joe's guys," he said. "He said three of our guys were hit over on Bleecker street just a few minutes ago."

"Hey!" I helped out. "Who got hit, Louie? Anyone we know? How bad?"

He shook his head and spread his hands. "Jeez! I don't know. The guy said he'd just gotten the word. Didn't know any other details." Louie paused and looked impressively around the room. "He said Uncle Joe wants us to hit the Ruggieros. Hit 'em good."

This time excitement had overruled any qualms Louie might have had before. The race of battle does that to men, even to the Louies of this world.

We hit the Garden Park Casino in New Jersey that night, eight of us in two comfortable limousines. The guard dressed as the elevator starter in the lobby of the Garden Park Hotel was no trouble; neither was the operator of the private elevator that went only to the Casino on the supposedly non-existent thirteenth floor. We herded the guard into the elevator at gunpoint, knocked them both out and ran the elevator ourselves.

We stepped off the elevator at the ready, submachine guns poised in front of us. It was a glittering scene. Crystal chandeliers hung from the high ceiling while plush draperies and deep carpeting helped to hush the croupier's sing-song, the click of the steel ball in the roulette wheel and the underlying hum of subdued conversation punctuated by occasional exclamations of excitement. It was the biggest gambling room on the East Coast.

A handsome man in a precisely cut tuxedo turned with the beginnings of a genial smile. He was in his middle 30s, a bit on the stocky side but dashing with jet black hair and bright intelligent eyes—Anthony Ruggiero, Don Gaetano's cousin.

He took in the significance of our entrance in a millisecond, spun on his heel, and made a diving leap for a switch on the wall. Locallo's machine gun ripped angrily, a staccato of violence in the charming atmosphere. Ruggiero's back buckled, as if snapped in two by an unseen giant hand, and he collapsed like a rag doll against the wall.

Someone screamed.

I leaped on a blackjack table and fired a burst into the ceiling, then menaced the crowd with my gun. At a dice table ten feet away, Manitti was doing the same thing. Louie, I could see out of the corner of my eye, was standing just outside the elevator, staring at Ruggiero's body.

"All right," I yelled. "Everyone be quiet and don't move, and no one will get hurt." Off to the left, a croupier made a sudden ducking movement behind his table. One of the other hoods who had come in our party shot him neatly in the head.

Suddenly, there was a deathly silence, with no movement. Then the Franzini men began móving through the crowd, cleaning cash off the tables and out of wallets, loading up with rings and watches and expensive brooches. The large crowd was in a state of shock, and so was Louie.

We were out of there in less than seven minutes and back in our limousines heading for the Holland Tunnel and our Greenwich Village hideout.

"Jeez!" Louie kept saying all the way back. "Jeez!"

I clapped him on the shoulder. "Take it easy, Louie. It's all part of the game!" I felt a little sick myself. I don't like to see men gunned down that way, either, but there was no point showing it. I was supposed to be tough. But this time the responsibility was squarely put on me, since I *had* set up that phony telephone call. I couldn't let it bother me too long. When you're playing the kind of game I was playing, someone is going to get hurt.

And by the next day, a lot of people started to ache.

First, the Ruggieros raided the Alfredo Restaurant on MacDougal Street where, contrary to orders, four of Popeye's hijack specialists had sneaked out to eat lunch. Two gunmen came in the back way, sprayed them with machine-gun fire as they sat, and left quickly. All four died at their table.

Franzini struck back. Two days later, Nick Milan, the aging *consigliore* of the Ruggiero family, was kidnapped from his Brooklyn Heights home. Two days after that, his body, trussed with heavy wire, was found in a junkyard. He had been shot once through the back of the head.

Then, Chickie Wright was shot down on the steps of his

doctor's office, where he had gone to get some pills for his hay fever.

Frankie Marchetto, a longtime underling in the Ruggerio operation, was next—he was found at the wheel of his car, shot four times in the chest.

The naked bodies of two of Franzini's men were found in a rowboat adrift in Jamaica Bay. Both with their throats cut.

Mickey Monsanno—Mickey Mouse—one of the leaders of the Ruggiero mob, escaped injury when he sent one of his sons to get his car out of the garage. The car exploded when the kid turned on the ignition, killing him instantly.

The final straw came on Friday when six Ruggiero men, armed with shotguns and submachine guns, stormed into the Franzini Olive Oil Co. By sheer luck, Philomina had just taken Popeye for his daily walk through the park. Four other men in the office were shot to death, but two women clerks were untouched.

We were putting the finishing touches on a bizarre plan of Popeye's to raid Ruggiero's estate in Garden Park when suddenly it was called off. Word had come that the Commission, disturbed as much about the sudden limelight being thrown on Mafia affairs as it was about the daily mounting death toll, had called a meeting in New York to arbitrate the situation.

Louie was excited again as we left our Houston Street apartment and headed for home, Louie to his bachelor pad in the Village, me back to Philomina's.

"Boy, Nick! You know, they're all supposed to come in! Tough Joey Famligotti, Frankie Carboni, Little Balls Salerno, all the big guys! Even Allie Gigante is coming in from Phoenix! They're going to hold the meeting Saturday morning."

He was like a kid talking about his favorite baseball heroes coming to town instead of seven of the most important crime figures in America.

I shook my head in disbelief, but grinned at him. "Where's it going to be?"

"The Bankers Trust Association board room up at Park Avenue and Fifteenth Street."

"You're kidding? That's just about the most conservative, established bank in town."

Louie laughed proudly. "We own it! Or, at least, I mean we've got shares in it."

"Fantastic," I said. I should have read those papers I had taken from the Counting House more carefully, but there had hardly been time. I clapped Louie on the shoulder. "Okay, *paisano*. I've got a date with Philomina tonight. You going to want me?"

He frowned. "No, not tonight. But on Saturday, each Commissioner gets to take two guys to the bank with him. You want to go with Uncle Joe and me? It might be a lot of fun."

Oh sure, I thought. Great fun. "Count me in, Louie," I said. "Sounds like a great idea." I waved and got into a cab, but instead of going directly to Philomina's, I went uptown to the Banker's Trust Association on Park Avenue. I wanted to see what it looked like. It looked formidable.

I went to the bus station, picked up my 17B kit and went back to the Chelsea to ponder my problem. The opportunity to be present at the Commission meeting was a stroke of luck, but I had to figure out some way to make the most of it. It wouldn't be easy. The Banker's Trust Association building was going to be crawling with Mafia hoods tomorrow, each fanatically concerned with protecting his boss.

It was Philomina, oddly enough, who gave me an idea that night after dinner.

She snuggled in my arms on the couch and yawned. "Do me a favor when you go to meet Uncle Joe and Louie tomorrow, will you?"

I cupped one hand around her breast. "Of course."

"Now, stop that!" She removed my hand. "On your way down to the office, would you stop and pick up a new hot water bottle for Uncle Joe?"

"A hot water bottle?"

"Don't look so surprised. You know ... one of those red rubber things. Whenever Uncle Joe starts shaking so badly he can't control it, a warm hot water bottle to put his hands on seems to help. He always carries one in that little rack underneath the seat of his wheelchair, so it's handy whenever he wants it."

"Okay, if you say so. What happened to the old one?"

"It's getting leaky," she said. "He's had it a long time."

I went down to the drugstore on the corner of Ninth Avenue and Twenty-third Street that night and picked one up. Then, later that night when I was sure Philomina was sound asleep, I got up and packed it carefully with plastique.

It was difficult to set the detonator and timer fuse in the water bottle, but I finally managed it. The meeting was supposed to begin at ten o'clock the next morning, so I set the timer for ten-thirty and kept my fingers crossed.

I was going to have to figure out some way not to be in the vicinity when that damned thing blew, because when it did blow, it was going to blow big. But I would have to play that by ear. As it was, I'll admit, I was quite restless in bed that night.

CHAPTER 16

Locallo drove Popeye, Louie and me from the office to the Banker's Association, and helped us unload Popeye from the car and into his wheelchair. Then, with Louie pushing the wheelchair and me walking alongside "riding shotgun," we entered the big building.

The board room was on the thirtieth floor, but we were stopped in the ground-floor lobby by two very efficient goons who courteously checked us for guns. Popeye wasn't carrying any iron, but Louie had a ridiculously small Derringer and I had to surrender Wilhelmina and Hugo. The two hoods gave me a numbered check for my weapons and we went on up in the elevator. No one paid any attention to the hot water bottle in the rack under the seat of Popeye's wheelchair.

Gaetano Ruggiero was already there, along with two of his henchmen, when we arrived in the large anteroom outside the actual board room. He stood tall and austere at the other side of the room, younger than I would have guessed, but with gray flecking the blackness of his sideburns. Hijacking and gambling were his major interests, the so-called clean crimes, but he was into narcotics, too, and murder was a way of life. It was on Gaetano's orders that old Don Alfredo Ruggiero, his uncle, had been killed so that the younger man could take over the family.

The others came in after us, each with two bodyguards.

Joseph Famligotti—Tough Joey—from Buffalo. Short, squat, with a dark greasy-looking face and a huge paunch that overwhelmed his waistband. He waddled as he walked, his suitcoat open to accommodate his stomach. He smiled benignly at Ruggiero and Franzini, then went directly into the meeting room. His two bodyguards stayed respectfully in the anteroom.

Frankie Carboni of Detroit. White-haired, prosperous-looking in a beautifully cut suit of gray worsted, sharp pointed gray shoes, a gray silk shirt, and white silk tie. He had inherited the old Purple Gang of Detroit and directed its bloodthirsty tactics into a ruthless but efficient protection racket that was the envy of all organized crime. He looked like a merry gentleman.

Mario Salerno—Little Balls Salerno—from Miami. Bird-like, a wizened little man, head darting back and forth suspiciously, deeply tanned skin stretched grotesquely over sharply defined bones, a big beak of a nose, and sharp-pointed chin. He had started with the gambling dens in Havana, moved to Miami, then stretched his bloody tentacles deep into the Caribbean and west to Las Vegas. At seventy-six he was the oldest active gang boss in America, but he wouldn't retire. He enjoyed his profession.

Alfred Gigante of Phoenix. As tanned by the sun as Mario Salerno, medium-sized, neatly dressed, hunched over, each move slow and deliberate, showing every one of his seventy-one years, but his startling blue eyes cold and piercing in the hairless head. It was whispered that his sexual pleasures ran toward little girls. He had made his way up the Mafia ladder as one of the first major heroin importers in the United States.

Anthony Musso—Tony the Priest—from Little Rock, Arkansas. Tall, slim, and graceful with a rich, benevolent look about him. Diamond rings flashed on his fingers and a diamond stickpin sparkled from his tie. He wore blue-tinted dark glasses that hid the acid scars around what had been his left eye before he lost it in the gang wars of the early 1930s. At seventy-one he was still the King of Prostitution, though he claimed to have made more money in stolen property than in any of his other operations.

One by one they filed into the board room. I could see them through the open door, shaking hands over the table, exchanging pleasantries. The seven most venal men in America. Popeye Franzini was the last one to enter, pushed in by Louie. I could see the hot water bag under the wheelchair as they went in.

The rest of us, about fifteen or so, stood around restlessly in the anteroom eyeing each other suspiciously. No one was talking. Then the door to the Board Room closed.

My fist tightened spasmodically. I hadn't counted on Louie staying in the Board Room with his uncle. Dammit! I had come to like the guy! But of course, you can't afford to do that in my business.

I was just turning to go, when the door opened and Louie came out, closing it behind him. He walked over to me.

I looked at my watch. 10:23. Seven minutes to go. "Come on," I said with assumed nonchalance. "Let's take a walk and get a little air."

He looked at his own watch and grinned. "Sure! Why

not? They'll be in there for at least an hour, probably more. Jeez! Isn't that Frank Carboni something? Boy, that guy just *looks* rich. And Tony the Priest! I saw him once when . . ."

He was still talking as we took the elevator down to the main lobby, where we collected our guns from the checkroom, then strolled out onto Park Avenue.

We had just crossed the street and were looking at the fountains flowing on the plaza of the big office building there when the explosion blew out most of the thirtieth floor of the Bankers Association Building.

Louie spun, one hand on my forearm, staring up as black smoke belched from high up on the side of the building. "What was that?"

"Just a guess," I replied casually, "but I think you just became head of the second biggest Mafia family in New York."

He never heard me. He was already running, dodging Park Avenue traffic like a football halfback, desperate to get back to the building, to his Uncle Joseph, to his responsibility.

I shrugged mentally and hailed a cab. As far as I was concerned, the job was over.

All I had to do was pick up Philomina at her apartment and head for the airport. I had the two tickets in my pocket and I figured that the two of us could use about three weeks in the Caribbean, just resting, loving, and relaxing. Then I would report back to Washington.

She met me at the door of the apartment, just as I let myself in, throwing her arms around my neck and pressing her body against me.

"Hi, darling," she said happily. "Come on in the living room. I have a surprise for you."

"A surprise?"

"A friend of yours." She laughed.

I went into the living room and David Hawk smiled at me from the couch. He stood up and came forward, his hand outstretched.

"Good to see you, Nick," he said.

HEALTH AND BEAUTY—ADVICE FROM THE EXPERTS